Finch
KT-383-651
020 8359 3800
OF TIME
JENNI JENNINGS
Illustrated by HANNAH PECK
30131 05759912 5
LONDON BOROUGH OF BARNET

Published in the UK by Scholastic, 2021
Euston House, 24 Eversholt Street, London, NW1 1DB
Scholastic Ireland, 89E Lagan Road, Dublin Industrial Estate, Glasnevin, Dublin, D11 HP5F
SCHOLASTIC and associated logos are trademarks and/or
registered trademarks of Scholastic Inc.

ISBN 978 0702 30441 5

A CIP catalogue record for this book is available from the British Library.

Printed by CPI Group (UK) Ltd, Croydon, CR0 4YY
Paper made from wood grown in sustainable forests and other controlled sources.

1 3 5 7 9 10 8 6 4 2

www.scholastic.co.uk

For Hugo and Oliver, my marvellous mischief-making nephews, with love.

1

TIME-TINKERING TREACHERY

It was a quiet afternoon at Malignant House.

Pa had been busy ahead of Felicity Square's Best Garden competition, depositing hungry slugs into would-be prize lettuces and tubs of begonias. After making sure his snail army was happily chomping away at the delphiniums and dahlias in the residents' cherished back gardens, he had come home for a nap before the start of his moonlight mischief shift.

To her delight – though you wouldn't know it to look at her face – Ma had been asked to create a

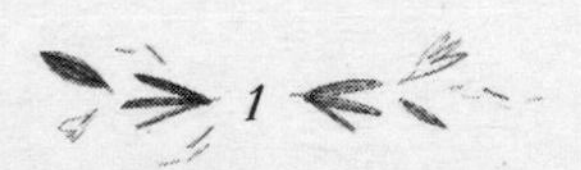

stink-bomb recipe for *Mischief Monthly* magazine. Three glass dishes sat on the worktop and were labelled: Horse Poo, Cow Poo and Pig Poo. Ma was enthusiastically thrusting her long, sharp nose into each dish, trying to decide which of the poos was the correct level of pungent for her recipe.

Malice and Grandad were in the attic working on Malice's history homework, a project on the Tudors. Grandad regularly played poker with one of Henry VIII's cooks down at Queenie Florus's Grandads Club, and he was only too happy to spill the beans with regard to the gluttonous king's favourite dinners – pretty much any meat cooked on a spit and the occasional swan, in case you were interested. Vegetables were for peasants.

Everyone was busy. Everyone was *too* busy to notice Antipathy-Rose, Malice's little sister, stealthily climbing the vast pile of swag which filled one corner of the dilapidated ballroom. Nobody saw

her scaling the jewel-encrusted mountain, up past the dusty chandeliers and into the vaulted ceiling. Nobody witnessed her swing her little legs to find footholds in golden goblets and diamond tiaras, or clamp her sharp teeth around ruby-studded sword hilts to lever herself higher up to the sparkling peak.

But everybody heard the sound of the gargantuan crash, as an avalanche of precious metal and priceless gems fell to the ground. The splintering, skittering cacophony of two hundred years' worth of stolen treasure hitting the ballroom floor echoed through the vast decrepit halls of Malignant House. If the place hadn't already been alive with ghosts, the noise

would have been enough to wake the dead.

The ruckus caused Malice, Ma and Pa to come running; Grandad floated because he was a ghost and didn't need to use his legs if he didn't want to. Malice reached the doorway and skidded to a halt behind Ma and Pa.

"Antipathy-Rose, my shark-toothed hellcat, where are you?" Ma screeched.

The ballroom was knee-deep in toppled heirlooms. The mountain of ill-gotten gains had been growing for so long, Grandad couldn't remember a time when it wasn't there. And now it covered the ballroom floor, rippling at the edges of the walls like a sparkling sea of swag.

The Malign family stood in the doorway, their eyes collectively scanning the ocean of riches for Antipathy-Rose. There came a *clink* from somewhere near the middle of the room, then another as something moved beneath the surface like a

crocodile, unsettling a silver cruet set and causing several gold bangles to jingle. The waves of historical loot began to swell and shudder, and then up popped Antipathy-Rose, an antique punchbowl on her head, her pointed teeth glinting in the light of a thousand diamond rings.

"Thank wickedness!" cried Ma.

"There you are, my mischievous maggot!" called Pa.

"What's that in your hand?" Malice asked her sister.

Grandad squinted at the orange orb that Antipathy-Rose was clasping in her hot little hands and said, "Oh, my shrivelled kidneys!"

"What is it, Grandad?" Malice asked. "What's wrong?"

Ma and Pa saw what Grandad saw and gasped. Slowly they began to wade through the swag towards Antipathy-Rose, calling out soothing things, as though trying not to alarm a fawn in a forest.

"Steady now, my little fungus," Ma cooed.

"Hand it over to Pa, there's a mangey-maggot." Pa smiled, reaching gingerly towards the tiny toddler. The sight of Pa smiling was only soothing to those who knew him best; to the unaccustomed it was a terrifying vision of crooked brown teeth and too much gum that seemed to swallow his whole face. "Come now, my slimy lugworm," Pa continued. "Hand the sphere to your old pa and I'll swap it for a nice juicy bone."

Antipathy-Rose looked unconvinced. She raised the sphere that had got her family all churned up and turned it, inspecting it in the light reflecting off the jewels which glittered around her. Malice looked hard at the sphere and then she too let out a gasp and clapped her hands to her mouth. Trapped inside the Amber orb was the unmistakable outline of a pocket watch.

"That's not..." Malice's words trailed off.

Grandad nodded at her.

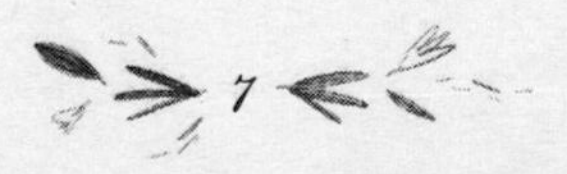

"Are you telling me that's Maniacal Malign's pocket watch?" Malice hissed.

Grandad nodded again.

"I thought it had been hidden somewhere safe," said Malice.

"It was," Grandad whispered. "Hidden in plain sight; the best place to hide a thing you don't ever want to be found. No one's bothered to sort through that swag pile for two centuries!"

Maniacal Malign was possibly the only Malign whose mischief was too malevolent for even the family to take pride in. He was known to have been something of a mad inventor. Maniacal's inventions were often more troublesome than triumphant, but even the most unsuccessful inventors get lucky sometimes. And that is precisely what happened with the pocket watch.

Maniacal was trying to create a pocket watch that could harness the weather; in particular, the power of fog. The idea being that when Maniacal found himself being pursued – which for a mischief-maker is par for the course – he would simply click the crown of his pocket watch and it would emit a thick fog, which would confuse his pursuers and allow him to get away safely.

Like most of his inventions, it didn't work. However, he soon found he'd created an even better mischief tool. Whoever the watch was pointed at when Maniacal clicked the crown became instantly frozen in time. And there lay the potential for the most monstrous mischief.

Maniacal used his pocket watch to turn the residents of Underland – land of ghosts, ghouls and

misfits – against each other. Let's say for example that Headless Mary was chatting amiably with Old Joe Fester about opening night at the Phantom's new opera, when along comes Maniacal Malign and, with a click of his pocket watch, he stops time. He plucks Mary's head out from under her arm and puts it in Old Joe's hands. Now, as everyone knows, you DO NOT UNDER ANY CIRCUMSTANCES TAKE ANOTHER GHOST'S HEAD! It's just not done. It isn't polite!

Well, you can imagine the to-do when Maniacal clicks his watch again to restart time and Old Joe finds himself with two heads instead of one. Everyone always says that two heads are better than one, but this is not always the case, especially not for poor Joe Fester.

Maniacal cruised around Underland with his magic pocket watch for over a year, turning neighbour against neighbour and friend against

friend. Eventually, Underland's general atmosphere of merry mischief was replaced by a maelstrom of misrule and mistrust. Underland historians refer to this period as the Pandemonium Pandemic. Something had to be done.

In an operation not much discussed in the Malign family archives, since it could be deemed "do-gooding", the family came together and hatched a plan to thwart Maniacal Malign's dastardly dominion over the dead. Tempestuous Malign and her sister Turbulence tracked their malevolent uncle to the Wild Witch Woods. Maniacal was industriously causing a rift between two covens by stealing the spell books from one and planting them in the library of the other.

The two sisters drew the witches away from war and into their confidence by calling a secret meeting and telling them about Maniacal's time-tinkering treachery. Ordinarily tittle-tattling on a

family member's mischief is absolutely forbidden, but desperate times called for desperate measures. With the help of the witches and the local cave mine ghouls, Tempestuous and Turbulence set a trap for Maniacal Malign.

When Maniacal overheard two witches cheerily discussing a new potion, he couldn't help but try to cause an argument. Maniacal slipped quietly through the trees towards the witches – but, just as he raised his pocket watch, the witches hit him with a stunning spell that rooted him to the spot. The Malign sisters took the watch from his frozen hand and hurried down to the caves, where the ghouls sealed the watch safely in amber.

Maniacal was taken before the highest court judge. He was forbidden from meddling with time and banished from Underland for one hundred and fifty years. Tempestuous and Turbulence hid the amber sphere and never told another soul of its secret

hiding place. Though many of the more meddlesome Maligns had tried their best to find it, its whereabouts had remained a mystery. Until now.

Antipathy-Rose grinned and ran her tongue over her needle-sharp teeth. Amber is a pretty tough substance, especially a ball of amber that is twenty centimetres thick. But Antipathy-Rose was a brilliant biter; she was biting through cradles and cables just two days after she was born. By the time she was a year old, she could bite through steel pipes. No one in that ballroom, dead or alive, doubted that Antipathy-Rose could bite through that sphere like it was rancid butter.

The family drew a collective gasp as the toddler raised the Amber sphere to her mouth. And then she bit down.

There was a crack as her teeth hit the hard crystal, which echoed around the ballroom and caused the chandeliers to shiver, and another as the sphere split

into two halves, to reveal the gold glint of the pocket watch.

For a heartbeat nothing happened. And then the sound of high-pitched hysterical laughter began to fill the creaking old house. It echoed down dusty corridors and bounced off the walls, gaining in decibels and delirium as it drew closer.

Malice and Grandad covered their ears. Ma and Pa waded frantically through the river of swag towards Antipathy-Rose. A wind blew up, forcing Ma and Pa back and knocking Malice's sister over. As the toddler toppled, the two halves of the sphere and the pocket watch flew into the air. A rush of stagnant morning breath swept into the ballroom, along with a ghost, which Malice knew from his portrait in the great hall to be Maniacal Malign.

With a triumphant shriek that was somewhere between a hyena and a howler monkey, Maniacal grabbed the pocket watch out of the air and disappeared through the wall with a *pop-fizz-zip*, leaving the rest of the Maligns frozen in shock.

Somewhere in the house a clock chimed, and the sound seemed to reanimate the Malign family. Antipathy-Rose turned on to her stomach and began to swim a fast front crawl towards her parents, who waded over to meet her. Ma swept her little daughter up into her arms.

"Oh, my poor putrid pomegranate!" she wailed.

"What about her teeth, Ma?" grumbled Pa. "Are they all right? No cracks or splinters?"

Pa had high hopes that Antipathy-Rose's gnashers were going to help him crack into safes and bank vaults when she was older. A cracked canine could be devastating for his future mischief plans.

Ma squinted into Antipathy-Rose's mouth.

"All pearly-whites still pointy perfect," Ma reported and Pa sagged with relief.

Ma and Pa made their way back across the ballroom, and Antipathy-Rose held out her arms for Malice when she saw her. Malice took hold of her little sister.

"What a bad ghost that was!" said Malice, and Antipathy-Rose nodded furiously in agreement. "Are you hurt?" Her sister shook her head in response. "Good," said Malice. "That's all that matters."

The toddler opened her mouth and began to point to her teeth. "You want something else to chew?" Malice asked and her sister giggled. Malice rolled her eyes. "I was saving this for your pudding," she said, pulling a wooden clog from her pinafore pocket. "But since you've had a nasty shock, I suppose you can have it now."

Antipathy-Rose beamed as she took the clog and began gnawing happily at the heel.

"I hate to say this," said Ma, with an expression of one who has just taken a swig of sour milk, "but you're gonna 'ave to go down to Underland to warn Uncle Vex."

Uncle Vex was a private Underland Investigator and all-round good egg, which made him extremely unpopular with the rest of the family, who really only liked bad eggs – the more rotten, the better.

"Ma's right," said Pa. "You're gonna 'ave to ask him to h–h–h – oh, I can't say it. By the fluff of my navel, don't make me say it!"

"You want me to ask Uncle Vex for his *help*, Pa, is that it?" Malice asked, handing him her sister, who had already whittled the clog down two sizes with her teeth. Malice brushed the wood shavings from her pinafore.

"There's no *want* about it," said Grandad. "Maniacal is on the loose with that pocket watch and we're going to *need* all the help we can get. We all know what happened the last time Maniacal was left to his own devices. He needs to be stopped. You'd best call on Seth while you're at it."

"That little mop-haired do-gooder!" spat Ma.

"Seth is my best friend," said Malice. "And a very good amateur detective."

Ma looked like she was swallowing down a bit of sick.

"I'm ashamed of her, Pa," she said, mopping her wrinkly décolletage with a wilted chard leaf. "I mean, I love her, Hecate knows I love our gal, but sweet mother of Circe, I'm ashamed of her Topsider ways. Is it something we did?" Pa shook his head and looked at the floor. "Did we not feed her

enough rotten sprouts? I should've known something wasn't right the first time I caught her with a scented bath bomb!"

"There's nothing we could have done, my mildew magnolia," said Pa. "She's just taking a bit longer to find her mischief-mojo."

"Oh, stop talking such rot!" said Grandad. "If it wasn't for Malice I'd still be trapped and spellbound in Underland, and don't tell me you weren't glad to have such a clever daughter when she outsmarted that highwayman who was skimming the profits off the Haunting Agency!"

Her parents looked peeved, but they had to admit that they had benefited on more than one occasion from Malice's quick thinking and helpful ways. They made grudging noises of agreement in Malice's general direction and shuffled off with Antipathy-Rose, whose clog was now gnawed to the size of a cat's paw.

The Haunting Agency was Ma and Pa's business; they provided nice Topside homes for despicable ghosts to haunt. Topside was where people who are alive live, and those alive folks are referred to, by the less alive down in Underland, as *Topsiders*. The Malign family were *Topunders*; meaning they could see, talk, and do business with the dead. Topunders could live in Underland or Topside and they generally chose to reside in whichever realm they could make the most money in.

It was true that Malice had a knack for solving mysteries, a thing she hadn't truly recognized until

Grandad was disappeared. Malice – with Seth and Uncle Vex's help – had not only found Grandad by using her powers of reasoning and deduction, but she had also been able to break the spell that kept him prisoner. Since then, she had become Uncle Vex's apprentice investigator (much to her parents' chagrin) and Seth had joined her in his capacity as amateur sleuth.

"Well, I'd best be off then," said Malice to Grandad. "Before Maniacal turns Underland upside-down."

"You take care, duck," said Grandad, floating up towards the ceiling. "And if you need my help, you just holler!"

"Thanks, Grandad," said Malice.

And, as Grandad's feet disappeared up through the ballroom ceiling, Malice left Malignant House and set off to find Uncle Vex.

PULPY COCKROACH JUICE WAS HER FAVOURITE

As Malice emerged from the shadow cast by Malignant House, the Felicity Square residents were already bustling about ahead of the garden competition, titivating hanging baskets and knocking signposts into their front lawns to direct the judges round to the backs of their houses. Malice waved and smiled but nobody waved or smiled back. Malice sighed and walked on to Affable Street, where Seth lived.

Seth was in the front garden with his dads, Bill and Pete, helping with the weeding.

"Hallo, Malice!" said Bill. "Will we see you later at the Felicity Square garden competition? We do love to see how the hoity-toity live! I hear the competition is pretty stiff this year."

Malice couldn't help thinking of Pa's slimy sabotage among the rose beds.

"Mmm," said Malice noncommittally. "It should be interesting."

Seth caught her eye and gave her a sympathetic look; he knew her parents wouldn't have missed a chance to cause some mischief amongst the marigolds.

"Can I steal Seth for a moment?" Malice asked.

"Only if you give him back," chortled Pete.

Seth rolled his eyes and tutted. "Dads!" he said.

The two friends wandered a little down the street. Children played football and tag along the paths, and mothers chatted whilst bouncing babies on their hips. The houses here were small and squished together and the cars that lined the street were old, and yet the people here seemed happier than the residents of Felicity Square. Malice wondered if it was being neighbours with her family that made them so sour.

"What's up?" asked Seth.

"There might be some trouble," said Malice. "I don't know exactly what kind of trouble, but keep your eyes open; you'll know it when you see it. I have to go and warn Uncle Vex."

"Are you going to tell me what's going on?"

"Would you believe me if I told you that one of my ancestors has a magic pocket watch that can stop time, and that he is going to use it to spread mayhem throughout Underland?"

"Absolutely," said Seth.

This was why Seth was her best friend. Seth accepted *weird* in the same way people accept that night comes after day, which was just as well given that Malice was ninety-two-and-a-half per cent weird.

"Good," said Malice. "Stay alert. I think my great great-great-great-great Uncle Maniacal is more likely to head down to Underland, but..."

"With your family you never know?" suggested Seth.

"Precisely," agreed Malice.

"What does he look like?" Seth asked.

Malice tried to remember Maniacal's portrait, along with the glimpse she'd caught of him in the ballroom.

"He's got dark greasy hair and a fringe that sticks

to his forehead in clumps," she began. "And of course, he's see-through in Topside."

"Obviously," said Seth.

"He's got a face a bit like a weasel," Malice continued. "With dark round eyes and a scrappy moustache that looks like someone who can't grow a moustache has tried to grow a moustache. Oh, and he's short and thin and he'll be wearing a waistcoat and breeches."

"The ghost's got style," mused Seth.

Malice laughed and rolled her eyes.

"I'll be in touch," she said.

Seth headed back up the road and Malice called "Bye!" to his dads, before making her way back to Felicity Square.

Admission to Underland happened on an invitation-only basis. This prevented Topsiders randomly dropping into the land of the dead. Since becoming an apprentice investigator, Malice had been given her own pass into Underland. She reached

her hand into her pinafore pocket and her fingers felt the hard, square edges of her Underland pass.

Malice turned the corner into Felicity Square and headed straight for the old oak tree. Its knotty trunk was as thick as the bases on some of Malignant House's towers, and its low-slung branches were gnarled and twisted like arthritic hands grasping the air. Malice pulled the pass out of her pocket, pressed her thumb over a small holographic star in the bottom corner, and waited.

Thankfully, Malice's neighbourhood was a hive of activity. The residents seemed too busy stringing up bunting and surreptitiously plopping buckets full of slugs over the railings into the communal garden to notice a door slide open in the old oak tree and a skeleton in a bellboy uniform step out of it.

"Greetings, Miss Malice," said the bellboy, dropping into a low bow.

"Hello, Charon," said Malice, bowing back.

"Where to today?" he asked, stepping aside and gesturing for Malice to enter the lift to Underland, before sliding in behind her just as the door swished shut.

"I need to find Uncle Vex, please," said Malice.

Charon nodded and consulted the myriad of flashing lights and labels on the inside of the lift.

"I do believe he's taking his morning tea at the Vengeful Brew," said the bellboy. "Shall I take you there?"

"Yes please," said Malice.

Since Malice had started frequenting Underland on such a regular basis, Charon had kindly taken it upon himself to make the literally hair-raising trip between worlds as comfortable as possible for her. As such, Malice now slipped her feet into a small pair of velociraptor ribcages, secured to the floor with bone bolts, and folded her arms through two woolly mammoth tusks attached to the wall behind her.

UNDERLAND

"Ready?" asked Charon.

"Ready," Malice replied.

"Very well, Miss Malice. Going down!"

Music began to play, and the lift began to plummet. Gravity pulled on Malice's cheeks, but at least now she didn't whip upside-down when she travelled. After a few minutes of feeling like her kneecaps were tickling her earlobes, the lift slowed and then stopped.

"Here we are, Miss Malice. The Vengeful Brew. Kindly disengage and stand on the exit."

Malice released herself from her bony safety harness and stood on a square in the floor.

"Thanks, Charon," said Malice.

"Always a pleasure," said Charon, and released the catch of the exit square.

Malice tumbled through the air and landed with a soft *kerflump* on a set of black velvet cushions in what looked like a broom cupboard. Malice shook herself and smoothed out her pinafore. Light spilled out

from underneath a door ahead of her, and, climbing over buckets and mops, she reached out and pushed it open into the Vengeful Brew tearooms.

The Vengeful Brew was situated in the Haunting Quarter, a part of Underland more associated with lurking than larking. Malice was relieved to find the atmosphere was as subdued as usual – this suggested that whatever mayhem Maniacal had in mind, he hadn't started it yet.

Malice weaved her way through the black-clothed tables and smiled genially at hunched goblins and secretive sorcerers, who eyed her warily over their teacups and spoke in hushed tones. Their acrimony towards her didn't bother Malice; she had grown up next-door to the Felicity Square residents after all. She was used to her presence being met with disdain.

She spotted her uncle's quiff wafting gently above his head, as he drank tea with Belladonna, the tearoom's darkly glamourous owner. Belladonna

smiled warmly when she saw Malice.

"Malice, daaaarling," she said, in her purring French accent. "Do join us. Would you like some tea? Or maybe a glass of freshly squeezed cockroach juice? It's got pulp in!"

Malice was tempted – pulpy cockroach juice was her favourite.

"Mm. Yes please," Malice replied.

"Hello, old girl!" exclaimed Uncle Vex. "Didn't expect to see you today. All grim on the home front, I trust?"

"Not exactly," said Malice.

"Don't tell me Pa found your school report?"

Malice's school reports were consistently outstanding, which meant she had to hide them from her parents so as not to upset them.

"No," said Malice, sliding into a chair across from her uncle and wondering how much she should say in front of Belladonna. "We had a visit today from a relative."

"Oh, really?" said Uncle Vex, shovelling a cinnamon bug-bun into his mouth. "Who's that then? Cousin Loki back from his travels, is he? I hear he's been causing a bit of a stink in Las Vegas."

“Er, no, it isn’t him. It’s someone I only just met today. Although I’m not sure it could be described as an actual meeting, more of a swooping and a stealing.” She took a deep breath. “His name is Maniacal.”

Belladonna’s teacup slipped from her fingers and rolled beneath the table; hot tea steamed up from the carpet. Uncle Vex chocked on his bug-bun and Malice had to jump up and thump him hard on the back to dislodge it. Belladonna had turned alabaster pale and she dabbed vaguely at her ballgown with a black lace handkerchief.

“I think,” Belladonna began, in a voice that was a mere wisp of its usual vivacity, “I think I need some air. Please excuse me.”

Belladonna stood unsteadily, and Uncle Vex jumped to her aid.

"Thank you, Vex," she said. Then, turning to Malice, she said, "Be careful. This ghost of whom you speak is bad, and not in a good way."

The many layers of her black satin ballgown whispered like dried leaves being dusted along in a breeze as Belladonna swept out of sight.

Uncle Vex had recovered himself and sat back down at the table. He took a long drink of something violently green in his teacup.

"Is Belladonna OK?" asked Malice.

"Oh, she'll be fine," said Uncle Vex airily, waving his arm in the air. "She's harder than diamonds. You just took her by surprise is all." Uncle Vex brought his voice down to a whisper. "Belladonna was around during the Pandemonium Pandemic," he said. "Those were dark times in Underland. Most ghosts have done their best to try and forget them. Now then. You need to write down the precise details of what happened. We can't risk causing a panic by speaking about it."

Uncle Vex passed his notebook across the table, and Malice began to write out everything that had happened before, during and directly after the altercation with Maniacal Malign. When she was finished, Uncle Vex read her notes, nodding his head sagely and mopping his brow occasionally with his pocket handkerchief.

"What we need to do now is observe," said Uncle Vex.

"Observe what?" asked Malice.

"Everything," said Uncle Vex. "We don't know where or when or in what dastardly fashion Maniacal's mania will manifest. Therefore, we must observe the normal routines of the Underlanders and be watchful for things that appear, for want of a better word, *fishy*!"

Easier said than done! Malice thought to herself. There were two important things that Malice had learned during her time as an apprentice; the first

was that *nothing* in Underland was *normal*, and the second was that *everything* that went on there was *fishy*. Malice supposed that the only way to approach this problem was to be vigilant for occurrences that appeared to be greater in their *fishiness* than usual.

Malice and Uncle Vex began their observations by wandering around the Haunting Quarter.

"Just act casual," said Uncle Vex, though Malice felt that his constant hat-tipping and calling out "Top of the morning to you!" to the hooded creatures who lurked in the shadowy alleys was not exactly casual behaviour.

Nothing appeared to be out of place; the residents were furtive and the shopkeepers unwelcoming as usual.

As they passed out of the Haunting Quarter and into the Shadow District, things continued to feel normal – that is to say, normal by Underland standards.

The jolly sounds of sea shanties being sung by rowdy ghosts spilled out from the pubs. Ghostly horse and carriages *click-clacked* along the cobbled streets, the drivers shaking their fists merrily at the urchins who danced out in front of them as they made off with some toff's coinage.

By the time they reached Gibbet Square, with its noisy street hawkers and eager shoppers picking their way through the sewage-lined streets, Malice was beginning to wonder if Maniacal had decided to hang up his trouble-making hat.

They sat down on a bench by the Bloody River, each with a steaming paper cup of witches' brew.

Uncle Vex was pulling chunks of mouldy loaf and throwing them at a family of Great Auks swimming nearby. "Well, I must say," he quipped, "I'm rather pleasantly surprised at the lack of trouble we've encountered. Perhaps old Maniacal has had enough of causing mayhem and has taken himself off to

Terror Island for a spot of the old R&R."

Malice nodded.

"Maybe," she said. But something in the distance had caught her eye; a small brown cloud was coming their way.

She squinted and held her hand up to shield her eyes. It was high noon in Underland, which was the time when the glow-worms that lit the earthen sky above their heads pulsed their brightest, as they wiggled in and out of the tangle of roots that formed a ceiling over the land of the dead. The cloud drifted nearer.

"What's that?" she asked, pointing.

"Eh?" Uncle Vex was distracted by a baby vulture that seemed intent on pulling the laces out of his shoes.

The cloud, Malice realized, was not a cloud at all. As it reached her head and began to circle around her, Malice saw that it was in fact a flutter of moths.

But these were no ordinary moths; their bodies were brittle and flaking and their wings were so gossamer thin as to be completely see-through, with tiny veins running through them like leaf skeletons. Uncle Vex looked up from his altercation with the vulture and exclaimed, "Oh my!"

Malice closed her eyes and listened. One of her magical gifts as a Topunder was that she could communicate with creatures that came out at night – bats and foxes and the like. She had a particular affinity for moth whispering, which meant Malice could enjoy two-way conversations with them.

She had also enjoyed some success with teaching Seth to moth whisper, which Grandad told her was most unusual since Topsiders couldn't usually learn Underland magic. But Seth was as unusual a Topsider as Malice was a peculiar Topunder; Malice supposed that was why they were such good friends.

The moths finished whispering their message into Malice's ears and she felt her blood run cold. As the tiny messengers disappeared up into the the glow-worm sky, Malice turned to her uncle.

"That was a message from Seth," Malice said. "The reason it's so calm in Underland is because Maniacal isn't in Underland. Maniacal is Topside and he's raising merry hell at the Felicity Square Best Garden Competition!'

The Building Was Mostly Used to Keep the Corpses Fresh

Malice and Uncle Vex stepped back out of the old oak tree and into what could only be described as mayhem.

Seth had come to meet them. "When you said *stay alert*, was this the sort of thing you wanted me to watch out for?" he asked, waving his arms to encompass the scenes of bedlam unfolding all over Felicity Square.

"Yes," said Malice absently, as she tried to

take in what was happening in the usually sedate neighbourhood. "Yes, this is the sort of thing."

Malice had never seen so much unrest in Felicity Square – not even the time Ma had shaken fart powder all over the burgers at the residents' summer BBQ, or the time Pa had swapped all the chocolate in the Easter Egg Hunt for rotten boiled eggs.

People were running hither and thither, with apparently no motive other than shouting at invisible perpetrators. A Bentley, a Jaguar and a Rolls-Royce had been inexplicably turned upside down, their wheels turning slowly of their own accord, while their owners shouted accusations at one another. Mrs Prig clutched her pearls in one hand whilst the other was plunged through the face of a large portrait painted in oils. The frame swung jauntily from Mrs Prig's arm, while Ms Vulgarian – whose portrait it was – teetered towards her in stiletto heels and leather trousers – not her own – which squeaked as she walked, pointing a

26
29
28
156
BIN

manicured finger at her bewildered neighbour.

"You've ruined my family portrait!" screeched Ms Vulgarian.

"Well, you're wearing my leather trousers!" retorted Mrs Prig.

"Not out of choice, I can assure you. They just turned up on my legs," Ms Vulgarian protested.

"Just as my fist found itself through the middle of your portrait!" Mrs Prig shouted defiantly.

At this point with neither one believing the other's innocence, the two women collided in a whirlwind scuffle of pearls and false nails.

"This is nothing!" said Seth. "You should see what's going on at the garden competition!"

Malice and Uncle Vex followed Seth down a shingled alleyway which led to the residents' back gardens. Mr Snoot's garden – his pride and joy – had been destroyed: literally blown up with TNT. They watched as he followed a fine wire from the centre

of the crater (which used to be his garden) all the way to his neighbour's house, his bald head pulsating with rage. Meanwhile, his neighbour, Mr Plummy, was looking confusedly down at his hands which held the detonator and mumbling, "But it wasn't me. I don't know how this got here. I'm a member of Greenpeace!"

In the garden next door, two police officers were scratching their heads as they tried to fathom how Mr Parvenu, a kind, elderly gentleman with a walking frame, had managed to uproot every plant and shrub from his neighbour's garden and deposit them on his roof, some five storeys up. Mr Parvenu chuckled in wonder and patted the shovel leaning up against his walking frame.

"You there!" Ms Egotist pointed at Uncle Vex. "You're one of the judges, aren't you? Come with me this instant!" she demanded.

Clearly Uncle Vex's sharp suit had misled her. He dutifully followed, as did Malice and Seth. Ms Egotist led the way to her back garden – or at least, what had once been her back garden. Now it was pancake flat. Everything, the flowers, bushes, vegetable garden, even the ornamental cherry tree had been squished. The garden looked like a giant canvas with multicoloured paint splattered all over it.

At the far end, Mrs Grundy sat bemusedly clutching her knitting in the cab of the steamroller which had ironed her neighbour's garden. The chimney of the steamroller gently chuffed out smoke while Ms Egotist chuffed out obscenities and Uncle Vex blushed. He tried to cover Malice's ears.

"Never mind the rotten language," said Malice. "We need to find the rotten relative!"

The three investigators began to search the melee for signs of a pocket-watch-wielding maniac, but if he *was* still there, he was doing a good job of keeping

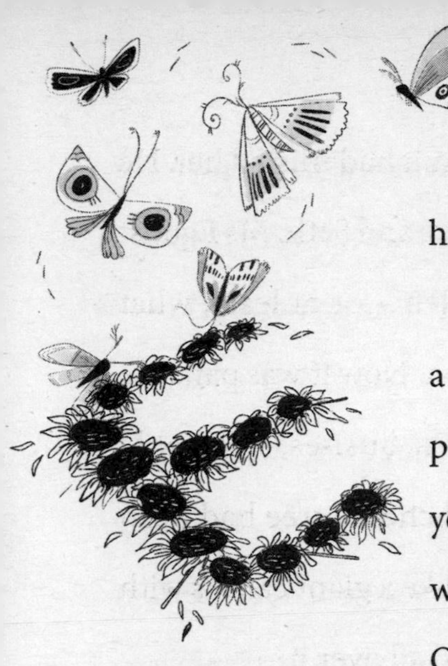

himself hidden.

Outside number nine, a police officer was taking photographs of something yellow on the pavement. Malice walked over for a closer look.

On the ground, made from what Malice deduced were the heads of Dr Ritzy's prize sunflowers, was a letter *E*.

"Do you know who made that?" Malice asked.

"Nope," said the police officer. "Do you?"

"No," said Malice. "Odd though, isn't it?"

"No more odd than the elephant currently stuck in the bathroom at number six," replied the officer sagely. "In fact, I shouldn't wonder if this 'E' relates to that very elephant."

Since Malice was now officially an apprentice investigator, she made sure she was never without a

E.

notebook and pen. She even kept one in her pyjamas because you just never knew. Now, Malice drew an "E" in her notebook and put it back in her pocket.

She had just reached Uncle Vex and Seth when she noticed a figure wearing a full-length cloak and hood, which appeared to be giving off smoke, looming towards them. When the figure reached them, it pulled back its hood just far enough for Malice to see that it was Lilith the vampire.

Uncle Vex leaped into action.

"Oh, you poor dear woman," he exclaimed. "Let's get you out of this sunlight and into some shade."

He put his arm around the delicately smouldering vampire and led her to a spot in full shade at the farthest corner of the communal garden in the square. Once in the safety of the shadows, Lilith pulled back her hood properly.

"We neeb you. Heeth bown in Unberlamb," said Lilith. "Heeth cauthing panbemonium!"

Someone had stolen Lilith's teeth. Stealing a vampire's teeth was the worst possible outrage you could cause a vampire. And there was only one ghost with the audacity to pull a stunt like that.

"Maniacal!" said Malice and Uncle Vex together.

Seth was staring at the toothless vampire with a goofy smile on his face. He didn't seem to have heard any of the conversation at all.

"You're a vampire," he said dreamily.

Malice looked from Lilith to Seth.

"Have you glamoured my friend?" she asked.

Lilith shrugged. "Ith not my faulb," she protested. "Heeth a Thopthider, Thopthiderth are authomathically glamoured by vampireth!"

"We need to go," said Uncle Vex.

"We can't leave Seth like this," said Malice. "Look at him!"

Seth was picking blades of grass, leaves and twigs off the floor and offering them to Lilith as gifts. In fairness to Lilith – who was a vegan vampire and had no intention of drinking Seth's blood, glamoured or not – she took the strange gifts from Seth with good grace and looked suitably awkward at the attention.

"No, you're quite right," said Uncle Vex. He pulled a black card attached to a lanyard out of his pocket, which had *Visitor* written on it, and fastened it around Seth's neck.

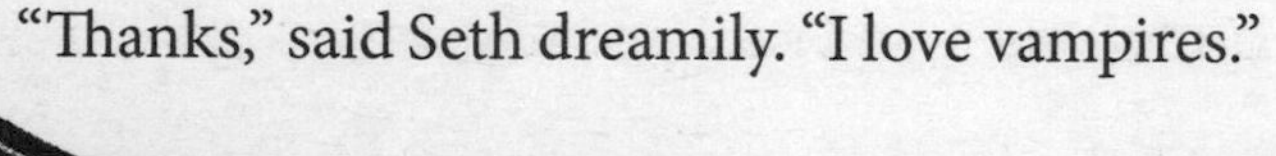

"Thanks," said Seth dreamily. "I love vampires."

"Belladonna will have a tea that can counteract the glamour. We'll just have to take him with us. Grab his bike, would you, it might come in handy. And whatever happens, it is imperative that Seth keeps that lanyard on him at all times."

"What happens if he doesn't?" asked Malice.

Uncle Vex's mouth pulled into a thin line.

"The visitors' badge is his proof that he is under my protection, and no Underlander will do harm to a Topsider who is under a Topunder's protection. Without it," Uncle Vex gulped loudly, "he would be at the mercy of the Haunting Quarter ghosts. And they aren't known for their mercy."

There was a clanking sound from across the way as Lord and Lady High-Hat chained themselves to the old oak tree – otherwise known as the lift to Underland – and declared they would remain there until the fire-brigade rescued their extensive and award-winning gnome collection from its branches.

Malice looked up into the tree, where many gnomes with coloured hats and fishing rods grinned out, and sighed. *What next?* she thought.

"We'll need another way down to Underland," said Malice. "The tree is occupied."

"Follow me," Lilith said.

"I'll follow you anywhere, fair maiden," Seth cooed.

Malice tutted and grabbed Seth's bike, which was leaning up against the railings, and wheeled it one handed, using her other arm to guide Seth, who was growing more dozy by the minute, as they followed Lilith round to the gardens of Malignant House.

Malice wasn't worried about being spotted by her parents because she knew Ma and Pa would be catnapping at this time, ready for tonight's mischief. She felt a little sad for them that they were missing out on all the mischief in the square; they would get a real kick out of all that madness.

Lilith led them silently around the edges of the

quagmires and swamps and through the pixie thicket until they came to the old brick-built icehouse. The icehouse was essentially a long tunnel built vertically down into the ground and lined with bricks.

In the olden days, ice from the frozen river was stored down there, supposedly to keep food fresh. But this being the Malign's icehouse, and the family not being fans of any food that wasn't at least mouldering, the building had been mostly used to keep the corpses fresh from their body-snatching business in the early nineteenth century.

Lilith pushed at the door and the gaggle climbed down a rickety ladder which led to the base of the icehouse. Uncle Vex carefully carried Seth's bike down, while Seth recited various love poems to Lilith.

"Roses are red, your lips are so blue,
Even though you are dead,
I can't help but love you!"

"Give me strength!!" groaned Malice.

At the bottom of the tunnel, a large hole had been cut into the curved wall for drainage. Lilith sat down on the ground and wriggled into it feet first, holding on to the top, as though she were at a water park getting ready to go down the slide.

"Juth relaxth," said the toothless vampire, before disappearing into the drain with a "WHEEEEEEEEEEEEEEEEE!"

"Where has my love gone?" asked Seth dreamily. "Halloo!" he called into the echoing tunnel. "My love, where are you?"

"You'd better go next," said Uncle Vex. His quiff was quivering, a sure sign that he was nervous about going down the drain. "I'll come down after you with the bike when I know it's safe. I mean, when I know *you're* safe."

It was clear that Malice would have to go with Seth, since Seth didn't know *what* was going on. She sat him down at the edge of the hole, then she sat herself behind

him and put her arms around his waist. She wiggled the two of them to the very edge and pushed them off.

The descent was fast and winding, and not unlike a slide at a water park after-all – if the water slide were in pure darkness and smelled of sulphur.

"I'm flying!" called Seth. "This is what love feels like!"

"Oh, for wickedness' sake," mumbled Malice. The sooner they got Seth to Belladonna, the better.

The speed whipped Malice's hair back off her face and the chill gave her goosebumps.

When they finally plopped out at the bottom, they were in a narrow dingy alleyway, in what Malice recognized – from its foreboding atmosphere alone – as the Haunting Quarter. Lilith helped them both up to their feet – Seth refused to let go of Lilith's hand – and Malice took a look around.

It was quiet here, but already she could hear the sounds of a ruckus out on the main road. Of all the

places she'd visited in Underland, the Haunting Quarter was the most subdued because so many of the ghosts who resided here were up to no good. It was a place of mistrust and nefarious machinations. The notion of a ruckus in the Haunting Quarter was a worrying one indeed.

Seth's bike clattered out of the drain and Uncle Vex followed soon after. He dusted himself down and pulled a lint-roller out of his inside pocket, which he proceeded to roller all over his suit until he was satisfied. He re-pocketed the lint-roller and pulled a small tube of hair-gel and a hand mirror out from his breast pocket and re-gelled his quiff.

"There!" he said, winking at his reflection before putting the mirror away. "Now we're ready!" He saw Malice and Lilith's expressions. Lilith would have kissed her teeth if she'd had any. "What?" Uncle Vex asked petulantly. "There is never an excuse to be ungroomed."

DESTRUCTION IS HIS MOTIVATION

The group kept their footsteps as light as possible as they picked their way along the dark alley.

"Is Seth still wearing his lanyard?" asked Uncle Vex in a hushed tone.

Malice nodded. Water dripped freely down the walls and ran in rivulets between the cobbles under their feet. The scuttling sound of small creatures with multiple clawed feet seemed to follow their progress. The closer they came to the main road, the more

pronounced the sounds of bedlam beyond became.

At last they rounded a bend in the alleyway, which offered a long, thin glimpse of the main street ahead.

The bright flashes of colour ahead might have been dancers at a carnival, but the colours weren't from costumes, they were the result of curses and hexes exploding on impact, and the cries weren't cheers but screams of rage.

"How are we going to get to Belladonna's without getting caught up in all that?" asked Malice. "You're all right, Uncle, you can make yourself invisible." Invisibility was Uncle Vex's magical gift. "But Seth and I might as well have bullseyes painted on our foreheads!"

Just as ghosts are obvious on Topside, due to them being see-through and a bit floaty, Topsiders are conspicuous in Underland due to their general aliveness. Topunders were only slightly less noticeable.

Uncle Vex pondered for a moment and then he turned to Lilith.

"Can you reverse your glamour?" he asked. "So that instead of inviting glances, you repel them? They don't need to be invisible; they just need to be not interesting enough to be noticed."

"Yeth," said Lilith. "I can boo bat. Children, get unber my cloak."

Lilith stretched her arms out wide and Seth and Malice tucked themselves inside her cloak. Malice could feel the energy of Lilith's repelling glamour pulsing out around them, causing the view ahead to quiver like a heat shimmer. They slowly walked the final few metres to the end of the alley and then stepped out on to the dangerous streets of the Haunting Quarter.

Ghosts and ghouls fought all around them. Black capes whirled in a blur of wands and glinting eyes, like the elaborate dance of a matador in the bullring. Curses zipped passed them, momentarily illuminating grotesque faces in the smoke; mouths

twisted into animal snarls, or demented grins, revealing crooked yellowing teeth. Spells fizzed over Malice's head and exploded in a shower of green and black stars as they hit their targets.

The four interlopers gingerly stepped over spell-melted cobblestones and tiptoed around ghosts, as they performed their danse macabre. Uncle Vex ducked down behind Lilith, "To protect them from behind," so he said.

Lilith's repel spell was working but it didn't stop Malice jumping and wincing each time a spell whizzed past her. Seth was entirely oblivious to the dangers surrounding them and said things like, "Ooooh pretty!" when a spell exploded in front of him, or, "Do you think a cape would suit me?"

Once, a ghoul with a humped back and long, dirty fingernails seemed to catch the scent of them. He sniffed the air through his crooked nose and lumbered towards them. Malice felt Lilith's arm

tighten around her. The ghoul muttered to himself as he sniffed about them. They held very still and Malice hardly dared to breathe. She hoped Seth wouldn't choose this moment to burst into a love sonnet.

"Alive," whispered the ghoul and licked his lips. "Fresh!"

The ghoul reached out his hand, but Lilith leaned forward and let out a low, menacing growl like a panther. The ghoul reared back like he'd been burned and slunk away into the shadows. Malice heard her uncle let out a sigh of relief.

"Come on," he said quietly. "The tearooms are just around this corner."

When they reached the Vengeful Brew, there was a *Closed* sign on the door and the windows had been hastily boarded up. A large letter "G" had been daubed in mud across the door. Malice quickly noted it down in her notebook.

"Belladonna!" Uncle Vex called through the letterbox. "It's me, Vexatious. I've got Malice with me. We need your help."

For a moment there was no response and Malice wondered if Belladonna had fled; Malice wouldn't blame her. But then, from the other side of the door came the *click-clack* jingle and grinding sounds of many bolts and chains being unfastened. The door was opened just enough for them to slip through before Belladonna closed and locked it behind them.

With the windows boarded up, the tearoom, with its chic black décor, was even darker than usual.

"He's back," said Belladonna, brushing past them with her familiar rustle of satin.

"Yes," said Uncle Vex. "We'd noticed. We want to try and stop him."

"Who hired you?" asked Belladonna.

"Nobody," said Uncle Vex. "As you know, Maniacal Malign in a family member. Unfortunately. And

therefore, the duty lies with us to put an end to his wanton destruction of society, once and for all."

"Strong words," said Belladonna, arching an eyebrow. "I hope you have the tenacity to back them up."

"We do!" said Malice, making herself stand tall. "But first we need to un-glamour Seth. At the moment he's a liability!"

They all turned to look at Seth, who was lying on the floor making carpet-angels with his arms and legs and singing:

"Twinkle, twinkle, vampire bat,
Creep and hunt just like a cat,
Flying through the streets at night,
Search for victims you can bite,
How I love you, vampire bat,
Please don't squash me like a gnat."

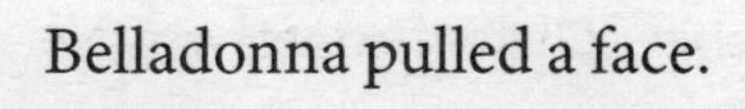

Belladonna pulled a face.

"Ooh, he's got it bad!" she said.

"He most certainly has," said Malice.

Lilith pulled her cloak about her.

"I muth get back to the Thadow Dithricth. Vlad will be worried."

Malice took the vampire and herself by surprise by giving Lilith a hug.

"Thank you, Lilith," said Malice. "Thank you for coming to find us on Topside, I know it wasn't easy for you. And thank you for protecting Seth and me. I hope you get your teeth back."

Lilith smiled a toothless smile as her cape became leathery wings, and before their very eyes, the vampire became smaller and smaller and battier and battier, until she was indeed, a small bat. Then, with a flutter of wings, she disappeared up the chimney in the large open fireplace and was gone.

"Don't go!" yelped Seth sleepily, crawling over to the fireplace and trying to squeeze himself up the

chimney after her.

Uncle Vex nodded his head towards the boy in the fireplace and said, "Could you possibly make us a pot of anti-glamour brew please, Belladonna?"

Belladonna sashayed over to the counter, where she began to drop dried herbs and flowers into a teapot.

"I don't know whether you are brave or stupid, bringing a Topsider to Underland, especially at the moment," said Belladonna. Her voice was soft yet reproachful.

"Didn't have much choice, old girl," replied Uncle Vex. "And besides, he's not a bad investigator, for a Topsider."

"Are you not worried that he'll freak out when the

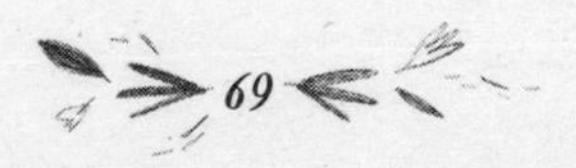

glamour is lifted, and he realizes he is surrounded by ghosts and ghouls?"

"Oh, no," said Malice. "This is basically Seth's dream come true. He's been badgering us to invite him to Underland for months."

Belladonna nodded. "I thought I could sense something not quite ordinary about him," she said.

Belladonna brought the tea things over and Malice poured Seth a cup of the brown, syrupy-looking liquid.

"Drink this," she said to Seth.

"OK," said Seth dozily, and he began to drink the anti-glamour brew. "It tastes like liquorice and ear wax," he added, smiling inanely.

Malice, Uncle Vex and Belladonna chatted in hushed voices while they waited for the brew to work. The fracas outside continued to rage.

"Do you know why there is a 'G' written on your door?" asked Malice.

"I think it stands for Gregor. Your relative hopes to

cause me pain by reminding me of the things I have lost." She looked wistful. "As if I could ever forget."

Belladonna didn't offer to expand on this, and given her expression, Malice decided not to ask. After a few minutes, the dazed and confused look on Seth's face began to clear and he glanced around the room.

"Whoa!" he said. "Are we in a haunted house?"

"We're in Underland," said Malice. "This is Belladonna's tearoom. You were glamoured by a vampire called Lilith and Belladonna made you a special tea to break the charm."

Seth sucked in a huge breath and Belladonna watched him anxiously.

"THAT IS AWESOME!" Seth declared. He was, as Malice had predicted, thrilled to be in Underland. "Belladonna!" he said, taking the tearoom owner's hand and shaking it vigorously. "It's so great to finally meet you. Malice and Vex have told me so much about you."

"All dastardly, I hope?" said Belladonna, smiling enigmatically.

"Oh, absolutely," said Seth. "Pure mischief!"

"Good to hear," said Belladonna, wrestling her hand away from Seth's.

"Right," said Uncle Vex. "Now we're working at full team capacity again, let's get our heads together. Malice, any initial thoughts?"

"The way I see it, there are three questions which need to be answered," said Malice. "One: how do we find Maniacal? Two: how do we catch him? And three: how do we stop him?"

"All pertinent questions," said Uncle Vex.

"To find him, I suppose we have to follow the mayhem," said Seth.

"When did things start to get maniacal around here?" Malice asked Belladonna.

Belladonna considered the question.

"Not too long after you left with Vexatious," she

said. "It started in the apothecary, over the road. A ghost *appeared* to pitch a potion at a ghoul, who hurled back a hex, which missed and hit a goblin, who cursed a mummy, who chucked a charm. And so it went on. Before anyone realized what was happening, we were in the midst of misrule. That's what Maniacal Malign does, you see; he creates anarchy by turning ghosts against one another. He stops time, sets up the scene so that it looks like one ghost has wronged another, and then he restarts time and watches the accusations fly."

"It's not just ghosts he turns against each other. Strange that he decided to start his time-tyranny Topside first," Malice pondered. "It's almost as if he's playing cat and mouse with us."

Uncle Vex's eyes twinkled as he picked up Malice's chain of thought.

"Hmm. You came down here to warn me; meanwhile, Maniacal was causing mayhem in

Topside," he said.

"But when we got to Topside, he'd already mischiefed and moved on, back down to Underland," said Malice.

"He's sending us on a literal wild ghost chase," said Uncle Vex.

"What's his goal?" asked Seth.

"He doesn't need a goal," said Belladonna.

"All villains need a motivation, surely, otherwise what's the point of all the destruction?" Seth argued.

"Destruction is his motivation," said Belladonna curtly. "The love of mayhem. He is the reason I haven't seen my sister in two hundred years." She leaned forward, and a sadness lit her eyes as she began to massage her temples with her fingers. "I was in love with a ghost named Gregor. We were to be married. Until Maniacal made me believe that my sister, Strychnine, had stolen him away from me. We fought. Strychnine begged me to believe that she would never do such a thing, but I had the evidence right in front of me; or so I thought. By the time I realized I had been tricked by Maniacal, it was too late. Strychnine had gone. I never got the chance to tell her I was sorry."

Uncle Vex dashed tears away from his eyes and blew his nose loudly.

"Did you try to find her?" asked Seth.

"I searched for a century," Belladonna replied. "But a ghost who doesn't want to be found, won't be."

Malice tried to imagine never seeing Antipathy-Rose again. The thought of it made her heart ache.

"What happened to Gregor?" Malice asked.

""We broke up," said Belladonna sadly. "Every

time I looked at him, I was reminded that I had lost my sister."

"We'll find Maniacal and stop him," said Malice. Belladonna's sad tale had made her more determined than ever.

"You must," said Belladonna. "It is not just towns his malevolence destroys."

Belladonna tightened the laces on Uncle Vex's roller skates and Seth attached the other end of the rope, which was tied around Uncle Vex's waist, to the back of his bike. They were going to have to move fast through the Haunting Quarter if they didn't want to get caught up in the trouble raging through the streets.

"Got your lanyard on, young Seth?" asked Uncle Vex. They had explained its importance to him.

"Sure have," said Seth. He lifted his visitors pass

proudly as though it were a medal.

Malice seated herself behind Seth on the bike and Belladonna got ready to open the door.

"Will you be OK?" Uncle Vex asked Belladonna.

"Dearest Vexatious, I have been looking after myself since before your great-great-grandad was born." Belladonna smiled at him indulgently.

Uncle Vex flushed.

"Yes, of course," he said. "Well then, keep up the good work!"

Belladonna pulled the door open and the three investigators sped out into the street.

5

WEREWOLVES ARE NOT KNOWN FOR THEIR GOOD HUMOUR

The streets were filled with smoke and the acrid smell of exploded curses. The taste was bitter at the back of Malice's throat and her eyes stung as she shouted directions in Seth's ear over the noise of the fighting. Seth swerved and skidded around warring warlocks and caterwauling crones.

"Where are we going?" called Seth.

"I want to drop in on some witches I know," Malice

shouted back. "They have a shop."

"They won't try to boil me in a cauldron, will they?"

"Not on a Saturday," Malice said. Seth laughed and then choked on a plume of blue smoke pouring out of a drain.

The Be-Careful-What-You-Wish-For Emporium came into view through the smoke and Seth slowed down and pulled up outside. The witches who owned the shop were a tricksy trio, but they'd helped Malice before, and she hoped they would again now.

However, on this occasion Malice was left disappointed. The shop was completely shut up. All the vials containing wishes for sale had been removed from the windows, so that only empty shelves lined with black silk remained on show. In the middle of the window the glass had been smeared with charcoal to form the letter "E".

"I wonder what that stands for?" asked Seth.

"Well, the witches left, so it could stand for *exited* or *exodus* or *evasion*," pondered Uncle Vex. "But it could just as easily stand for nothing at all and be the proverbial *red herring*."

"To throw us off the scent, you mean?" asked Seth.

"Indeed," replied Uncle Vex. "What better way to

keep your pursuers off your tracks than by sending them off on tangents?"

"I disagree," said Malice, jotting the letter *E* down in her notebook.

"I would expect nothing less, my dear," said Uncle Vex proudly.

"I think Maniacal's ego is far too big for him to want to evade us. He's got a two-hundred-year-old axe to grind – a metaphorical axe," she added, sensing a question coming from Seth. "I think he *wants* us to follow him. I think he wants Underland to know what he's got in store for it."

"Your mind is a chillingly suspicious place, young lady," said Uncle Vex. "It makes me proud to call you my niece."

A scrap of paper sticking out of the letterbox caught Malice's eye. She pulled it out. It was a note, burned crisp at the edges, but still legible. It read thus:

For the eyes of Malice Morbid Malign only.

Any other eyes can do one!

We're weary, deary, we need a rest.

This wretch has put us to the test.

Time ticks fast and engines whistle,

Our refuge lies in thatch and thistle.

We seek the commune of our kind,

An aberration there to bind.

"What does it mean?" asked Seth.

"It means, as I suggested, they've scarpered!" said Uncle Vex. "Can't say I blame them. Probably hiding out in a cave somewhere, till all this dies down."

"I'm not so sure," said Malice, folding the note into the back of her notebook. "Those witches rarely say anything that isn't worth further consideration. And they don't strike me as the kind of women to hide from anything."

"Well, they're certainly not here now," said Uncle

Vex. He swallowed and pointed a finger. "And we shouldn't be either!"

Malice followed the direction of her Uncle's gaze into the gloom and saw a pack of werewolves heading their way. Their fur had been shorn off, so that they were completely bald aside from their furry heads, and the culprit had adorned each of their torsos with a tutu.

Werewolves are not known for their good humour at the best of times, and they were especially tetchy about being made to look silly.

The werewolves prowled the foggy street, with teeth bared and red eyes glinting. Eight giant sets of paws padded stealthily towards them.

"I suggest that we leave right now this instant," Uncle Vex hissed and Malice and Seth nodded in agreement.

As the slobbering pack picked up speed, Seth began to pedal hard, with Uncle Vex being pulled

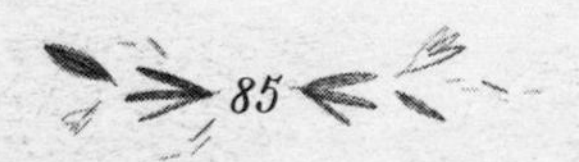

along behind. The werewolves gave chase, the sound of their baleful growls and piercing howls filling the air. Malice could hear the slap of many paws on cobbles. Uncle Vex yelped as the beasts took it in turns to lunge for his jacket.

"Faster!" screeched Uncle Vex.

It was impossible to see much at all. Spells flashed and exploded, and the multicoloured smoke from their impact mixed together to become a brown smog. Malice turned around but she couldn't see further than the end of the rope tied to the mudguard. She could only be sure that her uncle was still there at all because of his continual screeching.

"I can't see where I'm going!" called Seth.

"Don't worry about where you're going," yelled Uncle Vex. "Just make sure you get there!"

"But I'm worried we might be about to craaaaaaaaaaash!"

Malice felt the wheels of the bike leave the ground.

They appeared to be flying through the air, and for a moment Malice thought perhaps Uncle Vex had cast a spell to aid their escape. But then the bike began to drop, faster and faster, until, with a splash, they landed in a fast-flowing river.

The shock of the cold water took Malice's breath away, and she gasped and spluttered as she groped around for Seth and her uncle. Luckily they had landed close by one another and the water was shallow enough that they could stand their feet on the bottom – although the crunching feeling beneath her boots made Malice wonder just what the bottom was made of.

She looked around. Seth was shivering as hard as she was. Uncle Vex's suit hung limply on him and his quiff was drooping over one eye.

At the river's edge the pack of naked werewolves howled angrily.

"I s-s-suppose I'd be annoyed too if someone shaved off my hair and m-made me wear a tutu," Uncle Vex stammered, through teeth clenched with cold.

"I p-probably w-wouldn't mind it myself," said Seth.

Malice tried to raise her eyebrows, but they appeared to have frozen stiff.

"W-we n-need to g-get out of h-here q-quickly!" she said.

Despite the freezing water, the idea of climbing out into the jaws of the follicly embarrassed werewolves was not very appealing. Instead, they waded across the crunchy-bottomed river to the other shore, hoping that the werewolves nakedness would deter them from jumping in after them.

"D-do you know w-where we are?" asked Malice.

"Oh, y-yes," said Uncle Vex. "Th-this is B-Bone R-River."

"Why's i-it called that?" asked Seth.

"W-why do you think it's c-crunchy on the bottom?" Uncle Vex attempted a chortle but the cold stole it and it came out as a cough instead.

"C-c-c-cool," Seth said.

It didn't take them long to reach the other side,

and between them, they heaved the bike up on to the muddy bank. Malice and Seth managed to push Uncle Vex, who was struggling in his roller skates, up out of the water, and he in turn hauled out first Seth and then Malice.

The air was a little clearer of fog here; the sounds of mayhem still rang in their ears but it felt less dangerous. Their clothes were dripping, and their shoes and boots were squelching; Seth had to stop to shake a couple of bone fragments out of his trainers. Despite being out of the water, they were no warmer.

"We've g-got t-to dry off," said Malice.

"Agreed," said Uncle Vex. "L-let's see if w-we can find some sh-shelter."

The sodden sidekicks followed Uncle Vex along the bank and through an underpass, which led out into a spindly cobbled street lined with shops.

"Good news!" said Uncle Vex. "We appear to have made it to Shifty Row. At the very least, we can

SINISTER SEAMSTRESS
OP HAT & WAILS
SHIFTY ROW

purchase some dry clothes."

Malice knew that Shifty Row was *the* place for the discerning ghost to buy their clothes. It was where Uncle Vex had all his sharp suits made to measure. Ordinarily, two Topunders and a Topsider walking along the street, saturated in Bone River water, one in roller skates, two pushing a squeaking bike covered in duckweed, would have drawn some attention.

Today, however, was not an ordinary day on Shifty Row.

Maniacal Malign had clearly been wreaking havoc. As they walked, a ghostly window dresser, with a tape-measure around her neck, barged past them, hotly pursued by three shop dummies, who clearly weren't happy in the clothes she had chosen to dress them in. Outside Top Hat and Wails Taylors, two ghosts of vastly different shape and height were having a heated discussion over who had stolen

whose new suits; each gentleman was ill-fittingly adorned in the other's attire.

Uncle Vex led them into a shop called the Sinister Seamstress. Malice noticed there was a letter *R* made out of black velvet roses on the "Not Welcome"

mat. She stepped over it and made a mental note to write it down in her notebook when her hands had defrosted.

Inside, the shop was neatly-arranged, with the air of a fashionable funeral home. Several coffins stood upright along one wall. Their lids were open to reveal rails of suits and dresses hanging inside. There were three changing rooms, each one with a black curtain held open by a chalky white rib bone. Drooping headless floral arrangements adorned the counter, and behind that was a wall of wooden cabinets and drawers, and a doorway hidden by a black lace curtain. The quiet inside was broken only by the sound of a small fire crackling in the hearth and the noise of the furore outside.

The bedraggled gaggle shuffled over to the fireplace and huddled in its welcome heat, their clothes and hair dripping on the carpet while they warmed their hands. Presently, an austere woman in a black crinoline dress glided into the room, with the air of one who rarely meets her match.

"Madame Suture!" said Uncle Vex, bowing. "My friends and I are in need of your expertise."

Madame Suture looked them up and down appraisingly, making little clicking noises with her

tongue as she did so. Malice wasn't sure if she was sizing them up for outfits or for lunch.

"I am relieved to find that you don't appear to have been troubled by Maniacal Malign and his bothersome pocket watch," said Uncle Vex.

"He wouldn't dare!" boomed Madame Suture.

Malice could quite believe it.

"I have two skills which no one else in Underland can hold a candle to," the seamstress continued. "One is my nimbleness with a needle. And the other is an uncanny ability to never let a slight go unpunished. *No grudge is too little, no grievance too small, be assured, Madame Suture WILL punish them all*!"

Madame Suture's eyes glinted like steel blades. Malice gulped. She wanted to stay silent during this encounter, but her curiosity got the better of her.

"Excuse me," Malice began in a small voice. "But it seems as though Maniacal *has* been here."

Madame Suture drew in a sharp breath. An icy wind whipped around the room and the fire in the hearth flickered as though the air was being sucked out of it. Malice cast a sideways glance at Seth, who looked rooted to the spot with fear; he had even stopped shivering.

"I presume, impertinent young lady, that you are referring to the 'R' on the doormat?" Madame Suture said.

Malice swallowed.

"Yes," she squeaked.

Madam Suture looked impressed; terrifying, but impressed nonetheless.

"It is true that the watch-wielding wacko dared to darken my door. But!" Madame Suture barked the word out with such force that Malice and Seth instinctively ducked. "It is my opinion – and in my experience, *my* opinion is *always* the correct one – that the 'R' stands for RESPECT. Maniacal Malign

may cast anarchy upon the rest of Underland but Madame Suture commands his respect! Wouldn't you agree?"

Malice nodded emphatically, her tongue too trembly to form words. Uncle Vex, however, who by his own admission was a cowardly cowpat (Malice herself had witnessed him reduced to a doughy ball of dread by his own shadow), seemed unfazed by this sharp stick of a woman. In fact, he was beaming at the Gorgon-in-a-gown with something tantamount to hero worship.

"Monsieur Malign, the suit you ordered last week is ready for you," Madame Suture snapped.

"You are too despicable," said Uncle Vex, bowing his head.

Madame Suture clicked her tongue in a satisfied way and glided through the black lace curtain behind the counter.

"She reminds me of Mother," whispered Uncle Vex

fondly. "But without the axe."

Malice and Seth exchanged a look. Malice had never met her grandmother on her father's side, and she had always felt a little sad about it – until now. Malice pulled her damp notebook out of her pocket and wrote in an "R", then stood by the fire, turning the little book in front of it to dry it out.

A moment later Madame Suture glided back into the shop with a snazzy pinstripe ensemble, complete with shirt and tie. Uncle Vex let out a little gasp as he gazed at the suit and ran his fingers over the fabric adoringly. He seemed to have forgotten the perils they faced, and that time was very much of the essence if they were to find and thwart their unhinged ancestor.

"Madame Suture," cooed Uncle Vex. "As always, your work-womanship is exquisite." And he took the proffered suit, swooped into another deep bow and, remaining bowed, shuffled backwards into a changing room.

Madame Suture turned her gaze upon Seth and Malice, as they stood huddled and dripping by the fire, like a couple of street urchins. The sinister seamstress loomed over Malice.

"You are a practical girl, I see," she said. The sound of Madame Suture rolling her *Rs* was like an idling chainsaw. "If I were to ask you which one thing you deem essential in an outfit, what would it be?"

"Pockets," said Malice, without hesitation.

Madame Suture's mouth twitched into the barest of a smile and she nodded, satisfied. She turned to Seth.

"And now to you, young man, I pose the same question."

Seth, emboldened by the idea of new clothes, forgot some of his dread.

"I need to be able to ride my bike," he said. "And climb trees. But I've always

fancied going a bit Tudor, if you know what I mean?"

Malice rolled her eyes. Madame Suture raised an eyebrow, then snapped her fingers, and a measuring tape appeared in the palm of her hand. She sucked in her already hollow cheeks and began to flit about

the two friends so quickly that her movements were nothing more than a blurry mass of black fabric and pale hands. Malice and Seth found their legs and arms lifted, stretched and dropped, during what could only be described as a frenetic measuring process; it reminded Malice of the shark feeding frenzies she'd seen on nature programmes. When she had finished, Madame Suture stood back with an even more self-satisfied expression than her usual self-satisfied expression.

"I'll be back!" she said and disappeared behind the lace curtain.

Uncle Vex swaggered out of the changing room in his new suit.

"Well, I for one feel restored!" he declared, as he admired himself from every angle in the full-length mirrors. Then he threw himself down in the armchair by the fire and helped himself to a square of something green, dusted in glistening cobwebs, from

a crystal bowl on a side table.

"Mmm," he said, licking the cobwebs off his fingers. "Turkish Detest; my favourite!" He helped himself to another.

"Don't you mean Turkish Delight?" asked Seth.

"No, my dear boy, *they* are made with rosewater and orange blossom and the like. Whereas *these* beauties are made with cabbage water and turnip extract, and dusted in candied cobwebs. Try one!"

He passed the bowl to Seth, who gingerly took one and nibbled tentatively at a corner. Malice took a large dark green one and popped it in whole. "Yum," she said appreciatively. "Spinach flavour, my favourite."

Madame Suture swanned back into the room carrying two sets of clothing. She handed Malice a black long-sleeved dress, with two deep pockets at the front and another two at the back. Malice thought it was the nicest, most sturdy, sensible

dress she had ever seen. She gave a curtsy and said thank you.

Seth's outfit consisted of a doublet and hose, and a pair of voluminous shorts. Joy radiated out of him at the sight of it.

"It's awesome!" he gasped.

"Of course, it is!" barked Madame Suture. "Now, attire yourselves and get back out there and put a stop to Maniacal Malign's tawdry time torment."

Malice and Seth jumped to attention and hurried into the changing rooms. Uncle Vex reached for another Turkish Detest but Madame Suture slapped his hand away from the bowl.

"That's quite enough for you!" she snapped.

Uncle Vex smiled and murmured affectionately: "So like Mother."

After a while, Seth and Malice emerged, prancing and strutting respectively. Malice felt stylish, practical and ready to take on new challenges, and

Seth looked like he was about to take part in a theatre production; both seemed to be feeling mighty dandy. With all three investigators now dry and freshly clothed, they were turfed unceremoniously back out on to the street, and the door to the Sinister Seamstress was slammed behind them with vigour.

6

ONE CAN'T SOLVE CRIMES WHEN ONE'S MIND IS DISTRACTED BY WRINKLING SOCKS

"Where next?" asked Uncle Vex, just as a pie flew through the air and landed with a *splat* next to his shoes.

The pie's innards exploded out on to the cobbles. Malice bent down to inspect them. Something was not right. They consisted of a rainbow of fresh

vegetables: carrots, peas, sweetcorn and broccoli in a white creamy sauce. The steam from the mixture sent up a delicious aroma that made Malice's stomach growl; something was most definitely not right.

Another pie sailed over their heads and landed in the guttering of the building behind them. A rich filling of cauliflower cheese dripped out over the top.

"Since when did the pies of Underland contain fresh vegetables?" asked Malice. "Fresh *anything* for that matter?"

"Since never," mused Uncle Vex.

"I'm hungry," said Seth.

They decided to head in the direction from which the flying pies had come. Seth pushed his bike, with Uncle Vex's roller skates tied to the saddle, and the others walked alongside.

"That's Sweeney and Todd's pie shop!" said Uncle Vex. "Mrs Todd won't be pleased."

A small crowd had gathered outside the pie shop. Some ghosts were bent double, spitting broccoli chunks on to the ground. Others were shaking their fists in disgust. One was leaned against a wall, his head in his hands wailing, "four hundred and fifty years of being a rotten-meatarian undone with one mouthful of pie. Oh, the betrayal!"

"I'm ruined!" cried Mrs Todd, coming out of her shop and wiping her hands down her bloodstained apron. "That time tyrant has perverted my precious pies!" She wore a tall puffy toque on her head, from out of which her straggly orange hair was trying to escape. "All my pies are full of vegetables. Fresh vegetables, I tell you!"

A short ghost in chainmail clapped his hands over his mouth at the mention of vegetables and looked as though he was about to be sick.

"And as if that wasn't enough," an onlooking

journalist muttered. His lanyard said he worked for the *Daily Spook*. "Mr Sweeney has decided to become a pacifist and he's gone off to join the Cosy Grandad's Agency!" He finished scribbling in his jotter pad, snapped a photograph of the wretched scene, and dashed off down an alleyway.

A Viking ghost with a horned helmet and a plaited beard almost down to his knees asked, "Did you say *fresh vegetables*?"

"Fresh as the day they were picked!" wailed Mrs Todd.

The Viking fell to the ground in a faint. That was when Malice noticed a sculpture in the window of the shop, next to a plate of steaming pies. The sculpture was a letter *E* made from corn on the cobs.

She pushed past a queasy-looking ghost to take a closer look. Seth joined her.

"How much for a pie?" asked Seth.

"'Ave it!" groaned Mrs Todd. "Take 'em all, they're no use to me!"

Seth bit into a golden crusted pie and moaned with delight.

"Asparagus in cream sauce!" he exclaimed.

"Cover your ears, children!" cried a woman with two snotty-nosed children at her side. "Mrs Todd, I never did hear such language. This used to be a shop of disrepute and you've turned it into a – a – a *health food shop*!'

Two more ghosts fainted.

"Mrs Todd," asked Malice, taking a bite out of a mushroom stroganoff pie. "Why is there an 'E' in your window?"

"It's Maniacal, isn't it?" said Mrs Todd. "He's taunting me. The 'E' stands for the entrails that are missing from my prize-winning pies. Who wants a pie without entrails in it?"

"Not me!" snapped the disgusted-looking woman with the children.

"That's what PIE stands for," Mrs Todd went on. "Pastry. Intestines. Entrails. Now what am I left with? Pastry. Leaves. Vegetables: PLV doesn't exactly roll off the tongue, does it?"

"Unlike the fresh peas in these pies!" said a Roman centurion ghost snarkily.

"Wash your mouth out!" Mrs Todd shouted, and shooed him out of her shop.

Malice noted the "E" down in her notebook and dropped it into her new extra-deep pocket, while Uncle Vex and Seth tied bags of warm vegetable pies to the handlebars of Seth's bike. They were ready to go. *But*, Malice thought to herself, *ready to go where?* It seemed that Maniacal was always at least three steps ahead of them. And if they did catch up with him, what then?

"I suggest we go to the office and regroup," said Uncle Vex.

“And eat pie?” suggested Seth.

“Definitely,” said Uncle Vex. “We need to regroup and eat pie and see if we can work a plan. Besides,” he added, dodging as a curse of boils flew past his nose. “It’ll be safer in there than out here. Is your lanyard secure, Seth?”

“It is,” said Seth.

“Then let’s be gone. To the office!” cried Uncle Vex, and away they went.

It was dark by the time they turned into the road where Uncle Vex lived and worked. A gas lamp illuminated the door to the office, which had been decorated with what looked like a series of tiny belts with clips hanging from them. These strange items had been tacked to the door in two diagonal lines, to create the letter *V*.

Uncle Vex quickly began taking the small belts down and stuffing them into his pockets.

“What are they?” asked Malice, unhooking one of

the items from the door and inspecting it.

"A downright gross breech of privacy, that's what," grumbled Uncle Vex.

"Right," said Malice. "But what are they?"

Uncle Vex gave a long sigh.

"If you must know, they are my sock suspenders."

Seth choked on a chunk of pie as he tried to stifle his laughter.

"Sock suspenders?" Malice asked.

Groaning dramatically, Uncle Vex lifted his trouser legs to reveal one of the small belts halfway up each calf. The little clips held his socks up.

"I don't like my socks rolling down," said Uncle Vex haughtily. "One can't solve crimes when one's mind is distracted by wrinkling socks!"

Malice bit her lip and looked down at the ground to hide her smile.

"Now, if you don't mind, let's get inside and do some work," Uncle Vex grumbled. He unlocked the

office door and Seth and Malice followed him inside.

Once inside and seated around the large desk, each with a pie and steaming mug of stinging nettle tea, they began to discuss the letters that Maniacal was strewing around.

"I think the 'V' is a little obvious," said Uncle Vex derisively. "It stands for Vexatious."

"But why?" asked Malice. "What is he trying to tell us by leaving these letters everywhere?"

"I've told you," said Uncle Vex. "Nothing. He's trying to goad us, that's all."

"Goad us into doing what?" asked Seth.

"What you need to understand," said Uncle Vex, "is that anarchy is, well, anarchy! It is of itself disorganized. You're looking for a motive for the mayhem, but there isn't one; mayhem *is* his only motive."

"Then what should we be focussing on?" asked Seth.

"How to track Maniacal down, take the watch back

and hide it where he'll never find it again," said Uncle Vex simply.

"What about if, instead of hiding it again, we destroy it?" Malice suggested.

Uncle Vex shook his head.

"Unfortunately, it's not that simple. You can't destroy a magical item if you don't know how it's made. You need to understand the mechanism of the magic if you are to successfully disarm it. That's why it was sealed in amber in the first place. Only the magic creator can uncreate it, and Maniacal would never agree to that."

"What about if we blew it up?" asked Seth. "We could borrow a bit of TNT from Mr Plummy's stash in Felicity Gardens!"

"Or burn it?" Malice suggested. "Throw it into a volcano."

"Yes!" said Seth, punching the air. "A volcano!"

"That would never do," said Uncle Vex. "If we were

to destroy the watch we could mangle the magic, and the repercussions of magic mangling are grave indeed, especially where time is concerned. It could take us all back in time, or forwards in time, or even stop time permanently – freeze the universe as it is now, for ever."

"That's quite serious," said Seth.

"Couldn't we ask Tempestuous and Turbulence Malign for help?" asked Malice. "They thwarted him before. They might have some insider info that could help us."

"They went into hiding themselves after hiding the pocket watch, for fear of being forced by nefarious ghouls to divulge its whereabouts. There were those in the Haunting Quarter who would have liked that watch for themselves and would have stopped at nothing to get it back."

"What about the witches who helped them, then?" asked Malice.

"It's a thought," said Uncle Vex. "I'll quickly fire off

a couple of ghoulagrams to the Wild Witch Woods now," he said, opening his laptop with a yawn, "and then I think it's time we got some sleep. We're going to need our strength."

Seth yawned too and Malice followed.

"Can you let my dads know I'm having a sleepover?" said Seth.

"I'll do it right this second," said Uncle Vex, his fingers a blur as he clicked "send" on the ghoulagrams to the witches and proceeded to type a ghostmail to Seth's dad Bill. Bill and Uncle Vex were old school friends, and Bill knew Vex was a trustworthy sort; although he might not have felt that way if he knew that his son was currently in the land of the dead.

Uncle Vex pulled open the bottom drawer of a filing cabinet and stepped down into it. Malice and Seth followed. There was a chilly breeze in the stairwell and the stone walls radiated cold.

The stairs went down for one flight, then turned

sharply and rose steeply upwards in a spiral. As they climbed, the air became warmer and infused with scents of lavender and sandalwood, and the stone walls were covered in a busy floral wallpaper.

The lock clicked and the door at the top of the staircase swung open to reveal a circular room, lavishly furnished with bouncy sofas and scatter cushions, and views over the rooftops of Underland. The earthen sky was almost completely dark now that the glow-worms were resting, and the city below was lit by a spooky haze of gas-lamps and

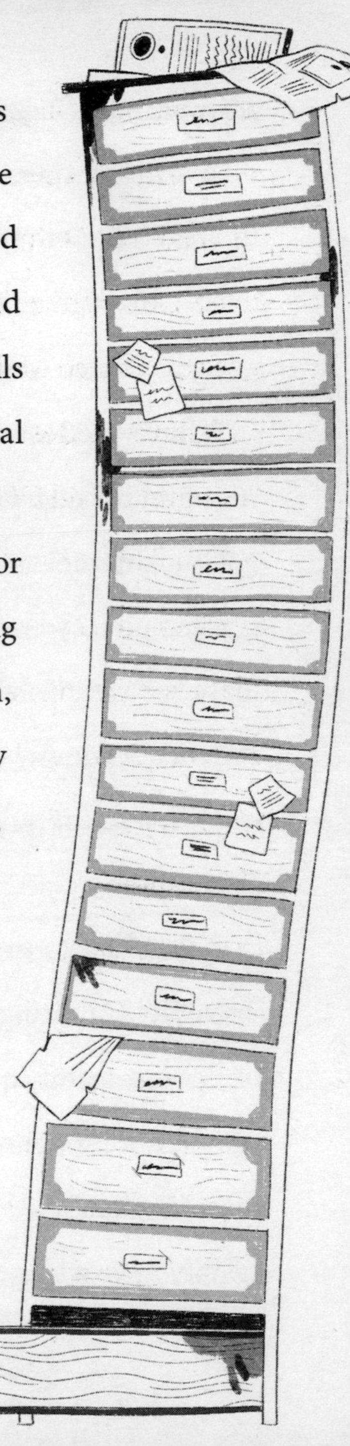

yellow candles flickering behind leaded windows.

"Wow!" said Seth, swaying slightly with tiredness. "If I had this view, I'd never leave the house."

"It's this view that drives me to keep Underland safe," said Uncle Vex.

Seth yawned loudly.

"Mind if I turn in?" he asked drowsily. "When I woke up this morning, I had no idea I'd be glamoured by a vampire, cycling around the land of the dead or chased by werewolves. I am well and truly pooped!"

"There's a guest bed ready when you are, old boy," said Uncle Vex, pointing to a door leading off the sitting room.

In the distance, spells continued to blaze, exploding above the Haunting Quarter like fireworks. Other areas were deathly quiet, as though hunkered down to avoid the mayhem. Malice yawned. She didn't know how long she'd been sat at the window watching the city below, wondering where Maniacal Malign

was hiding. *Where would he strike next? Were her family safe? Was anybody really safe while Maniacal was wielding the power of time like a weapon?*

She felt a reassuring hand on her shoulder.

"Come on, old girl," said Uncle Vex. "Time for bed. Worry is the worst whittler of wisdom. Rest your brainbox now and it'll be fighting fit for battle in the morning."

Malice looked around and realized that Seth must have already gone to bed. She smiled at her uncle and made her way through a door along the back wall, which led to the second guest bedroom.

Like everything about Uncle Vex, the room was stylish and the furnishings sumptuous, and it didn't take long for Malice to drop off into a sleep that the dead would be proud of, in the squashy four-poster bed.

TROUNCE THIS TROUBLESOME TIME TOMFOOLERY

When Malice walked into the sitting room the next morning, she found Grandad sitting at the table with Uncle Vex having breakfast.

"Grandad!" said Malice, throwing her arms around him and giving him a massive hug. Because Grandad was a ghost, he wasn't solid back in Topside, so Malice made the most of hugging him down in Underland. "Is everything all right in Topside?" she asked, suddenly worried. "Ma, Pa and Antipathy-

Rose are OK, aren't they?"

"They're fine, duckie," said Grandad. "Gruesome as the day they were born. I've come down because Maniacal seems to have left us another message. Though what his messages mean is any ghost's guess! We didn't find it until we'd cleared away some of the swag in the ballroom."

"What was it?" asked Malice, sitting down at the table. She helped herself to a slice of furry toast and spread it thickly with poison berry jam.

"It was a letter 'E'," said Grandad. "Made out of crushed amber crystals from the sphere that his

pocket watch was sealed in. It was melted into the ballroom floor."

Malice wrote the letter 'E' into her notebook. *Three Es,* she thought. What was the relevance of all these letters? She wrote them out in the order in which they'd been found: *E, G, R, E, V, E.*

"Penny for them," said Grandad, watching with a piece of jammy toast suspended halfway to his mouth.

"I'm just trying to work out what it all means," said Malice.

"Well," said Uncle Vex. "If it means anything at all, I'd say the 'E' in this instance stands for *extricated* or *emancipated*. As in, he's *extracted* the pocket watch from the amber sphere. He's taunting us with the fact that, despite our best efforts, he's got his watch back."

"I think there's more to it than that," said Malice.

Grandad took her hand and squeezed it.

"If you think there's something hidden in these letters, then there likely is," he said. "You're the best

puzzler I know. As good even as your nana."

Malice's nana was a witch. She and Grandad were divorced, but they were still friends. Nana ran a spa hotel in the Wild Witch Woods, called The Weary Necromancer.

"If you've got a hunch," Grandad continued, "you chase it down, my girl."

"Thanks, Grandad." Malice turned to Uncle Vex. "Did you hear anything back from the covens in the Wild Witch Woods yet?"

"Nothing yet," said Uncle Vex. "Which is strange because witches are normally very good at correspondence."

"I've been thinking about how to deal with the watch when we find it," said Malice. "We can't risk destroying it because we don't know how it will affect time. And hiding it is, as we've seen, a temporary measure. What about if we dismantle it?"

"But you've just said we can't destroy it, the magic

is too unstable," said Uncle Vex.

"We don't dismantle to destroy; we dismantle to diffuse and confuse."

Uncle Vex tapped his chin with his finger.

"I'm sorry, I don't get your meaning," he said.

"What if there was a way that we could take the watch apart and hide every single piece of it separately, all over the place, so that it would be impossible for anyone to ever find all the missing pieces," Malice suggested.

"I follow," said Uncle Vex. "And the idea has merit."

Malice could sense there was a "but" coming.

"But," Uncle Vex went on, "what you're suggesting would be a mammoth undertaking, involving many ghosts and ghouls, and I'm just not sure it's practical."

"And what are *your* ideas so far, Vexatious, me old pal?" Grandad asked.

Uncle Vex sighed.

"None as good as that one yet, I have to admit,"

he said. "But I remain hopeful that inspiration will strike. In the meantime, my sources tell me that Maniacal's mayhem has made its way through the Underland Market, Terror Island and Theatre Land. Shakespeare is spitting feathers – quite literally, so I'm told. I've got a map of Underland," Uncle Vex moved the breakfast things to one side and laid the map out flat. "I suggest we mark where he's been and when, and see if there is any pattern that may give us a clue as to where he'll strike next."

"I'll wake Seth up," said Malice. "He's usually up early."

"It's his first time in Underland," said Grandad. "There's a lot to take in, it's probably taken it out of him."

Malice knocked on Seth's door, but there was no reply.

"Wakey-wakey, sleepy head!" she called as she entered.

The room was quiet. Though the curtains were still drawn, the window was wide open, and the drapes flapped wildly. Malice shivered as she crossed over to the lump in the bed and gave it a shake. The lump did not feel Seth shaped.

Malice's heart began to pound. She was too frightened to pull back the covers. And then she saw it, hanging from the bedpost, Seth's lanyard. He must have taken it off to go to sleep. Without it, he didn't have Uncle Vex's protection. She swallowed down her fear and heaved the covers completely off the bed. *Oh No!*

"Uncle Vex! Grandad!" Malice yelled.

The door flew open.

"Oh, my perished pancreas!" cried Grandad.

"Oh dear," said Uncle Vex. "Oh, dear, oh dear, oh dear."

The space where Seth should have been was filled pine cones. Pinned to the pillow was a note:

VISITOR

Not nice is it, to lose a friend?

Now my despair you'll comprehend.

Nomadic, banished, bereft of treasure,

Nefarious plans became my pleasure.

Night after night of bided time,

Nemesis, you'll soon be mine!

Uncle Vex was the first to gather his wits.

"Every line starts with an 'N'. Malice, where is your notebook?"

Malice could hardly think straight. Poor Seth. Her best friend kidnapped by a time-bending maniac!

"Malice!" said Uncle Vex. "Focus. I know this is hard, but if we are to help Seth, we must understand what it is that Maniacal is trying to tell us. I'm sorry I doubted you when you said Maniacal was sending us messages. This note proves your theory; if this isn't a declaration of intent, I don't know what is! You were right all along."

Grandad guided Malice back out of the room and sat her down at the table.

"Come on, duck," he said. "Seth will be fine. He's a clever, resourceful boy and he doesn't scare easy. Now let's see if we can crack Maniacal's diabolical message."

Malice laid Maniacal's note in the middle of the table and then she pulled out her notebook. In a shaking hand she wrote the latest letter 'N' beside the rest. She looked at them.

EGREVEN

Uncle Vex came up behind her and looked over her shoulder.

"EGREVEN!" he mused. "What does that mean?"

"I think it's an anagram," said Malice.

"I'd say so," agreed Grandad.

"Right then," said Uncle Vex, rolling up his sleeves.

Each of them took a piece of paper and began to

write down variations of the letters.

"GREENEV!" said Uncle Vex triumphantly.

"I don't think so," said Malice.

A moment later, Uncle Vex slapped his pencil down on the table. "Solved it! EVERNEG! You're welcome." He frowned. "No, scrap that, of course, how foolish of me, it's EGREVEN!"

"The thing about anagrams, my boy, is that they have to mean something," said Grandad.

"It might mean something, in another language," said Uncle Vex hopefully. "How's your knowledge of Goblin?"

Malice, meanwhile, had worked it out. And as she did so, so the rest of the pieces of the puzzle fell into place. She wrote the letters out and pushed the paper over to Uncle Vex and Grandad.

REVENGE

"Got it in one, duck," said Grandad.

"Great Zeus!" said Uncle Vex. "You were right, Malice, there was clearly method to his mayhem all along. I had assumed that creating anarchy was in and of itself the only motive."

"But revenge upon who?" asked Grandad.

Malice pulled the folded witches' letter from the back of her notebook and read it again.

"It wasn't only Tempestuous and Turbulence who stopped Maniacal," said Malice.

Understanding broke across her Uncle's face.

"In the absence of Tempestuous and Turbulence, he is planning to take his revenge on everyone else involved in bringing about his comeuppance," said Uncle Vex.

"It was all in the shop witches' letter," said Malice pushing it towards her uncle.

We're weary, deary, we need a rest.
This wretch has put us to the test.
Time ticks fast and engines whistle,
Our refuge lies in thatch and thistle.
We seek the commune of our kind,
An aberration there to bind.

"They saw it coming. They've gone by train – *engines whistle* – to seek *the commune of our kind*, in other words fellow witches. *An aberration there to bind*, is clearly their intent to stop Maniacal again. And where do *weary* witches go when they need a *rest*?"

"Oh dear," said Grandad.

"Exactly," said Malice. "They're headed to The Weary Necromancer in the Wild Witch Woods."

"Your nana's hotel," said Grandad.

"Maniacal is going back to the place where he was defeated last time to exact his revenge," said Uncle Vex.

"I'm sure of it," said Malice. "I don't think it's a coincidence that he's filled the bed with pine cones. The Wild Witch Woods are full of pine trees."

"If only I'd seen it sooner!" said Uncle Vex in frustration.

"Don't be so hard on yourself," said Grandad. "Maniacal has been leading you a right merry dance!"

"Do you think he'll hurt Seth?" Malice asked. Her stomach churned with worry for her best friend.

"He's using Seth as bait," said Uncle Vex, not unkindly. "It wouldn't do him any good to harm him."

"But why is he baiting us?" asked Malice. "We didn't have anything to do with his capture last time. Seth isn't even related to Maniacal!"

Grandad had been poring over Maniacal's note and the marks of his mayhem on the map.

"Maniacal isn't only a maniac," said Grandad. "He's a megalomaniac! He wants an audience. A public revenge that will go down in history. All of this has

just been attention-seeking for the grand event."

"What better way to draw attention to yourself than to cause chaos everywhere you go and then kidnap a Topsider. The whole of Underland will be talking about it," said Uncle Vex. "It's pretty ingenious, in an evil sort of way."

Malice pushed the butterflies in her stomach down and steadied her nerve. Her determination to stop Maniacal Malign's reign of time-trickery had been strong before. But now that he had kidnapped her best friend, she felt a fiery resolve running through her veins and an iron fortitude filling her chest. And an almost overwhelming urge to punch that time-meddler right on the nose!

"Well," said Malice, standing up. "Now we know which way we're headed. We're going to the Wild Witch Woods to save Seth, protect Nana and trounce this troublesome time tomfoolery!"

"I'm with you!" said Uncle Vex.

"I should hope so," said Malice. "I'm not going by myself!"

"I'm coming too," said Grandad. "If Nana's in danger, I want to help."

Malice took Grandad's arm and rested her head on his shoulder, revelling – just for a moment – in how nice it was to be able to cuddle him.

"I know you want to help Nana," she said. "But Nana is a great witch, and she'll have me and Uncle Vex and probably half the witches in Underland looking out for her. Ma and Pa and Antipathy-Rose are in Topside alone, and you know that they aren't half so good at getting themselves out of trouble as they are getting into it."

"You want me to man the fort in Topside," said Grandad.

"I'd feel better knowing you were there to protect them," said Malice.

Grandad pulled Malice into a hug.

"Your wits are as sharp as your heart is big," said Grandad. "You make me proud every day."

He shook hands with Uncle Vex.

"Take care my boy," said Grandad. "And keep each other safe."

Grandad left with a cheery wave and the two remaining investigators got ready to catch a train to the Wild Witch Woods.

8

NO ONE BATS AN EYELID IF YOU HAVE BATS IN YOUR HAIR

Underland Central Station was even more packed than usual. It seemed every ghost wanted to escape the city and the madness within it. The steam engines lined up against the many platforms huffed and puffed as though annoyed at being kept waiting.

Malice could have cried when she saw the length of the queue for tickets. Ghosts and ghouls hovered, cheekbone by jowl, as they waited in disorderly lines,

which snaked out of the station and were swallowed into the murky clouds of exploded hexes. *We'll never get there at this rate!* Malice thought. She could feel her anxiety rising. Seth was her best friend and he needed her help; she needed to get to the Wild Witch Woods.

"I took the liberty of purchasing these."

Belladonna glided out of the shadows and handed Malice and Vex a ticket each.

"The ghost train for the Wild Witch Woods leaves in three minutes," Belladonna continued, while Malice and Uncle Vex gawped at her in surprise. "I suggest we are on it."

“We?” said Malice, finding her voice.

“The witches have been leaving the city in droves, which means they are on to something. And when my sources informed me that you too were headed for the Wild Witch Woods, my mind was made up. Maniacal Malign tore a rift between my sister and me that I have never been able to fix. I want to help you stop him. For sisters everywhere.”

Malice wasn’t sure who or what Belladonna’s *sources* were, but she was pleased that the glamorous ghost would be joining them in their quest.

“Glad to have you on the team,” said Uncle Vex. “Lead the way!”

They followed Belladonna on to the train, squeezing down the corridors past agitated witches and through several carriages, until finally they reached their compartment. Two plump witches and a third, the shape of a pipe cleaner, sat amongst a hotchpotch of carpet bags, broomsticks and cauldrons.

"Wild Witch Woods, is it?" said one of the witches, as they took their seats in the crowded compartment.

"Yes," said Malice. Uncle Vex stayed quiet. Witches made him nervous. Many things made Uncle Vex nervous, but witches in particular brought out the coward in him.

"Us too," said the witch. "All the witches in this part of Underland are going there. We've been called to a coven convention. Got to figure out what to do about Maniacal Malign once and for all!"

"Do you have a plan?" Malice asked, wondering whether she and Uncle Vex might not have to worry about stopping Maniacal if the witches had it hand.

"Not exactly," said the pipe-cleaner witch. "The convention is being held at The Weary Necromancer. It's a spa-hotel. Lovely spot. We'll put our cauldrons together and see what happens."

"That's my Nana's hotel," said Malice.

The witches looked impressed and Malice felt quite proud.

"So, you're Mesmerist's granddaughter!" exclaimed one of the plump witches. "The one who likes bathing."

Malice grinned as the witches inspected her. She half expected them to lean across and give her a sniff. Malice saw Belladonna, who had her head buried in a book called *One Hundred Plants to Make You Dead*, supress a smile.

Uncle Vex pulled his fedora over his face and went to sleep. Belladonna read her book and the witches incanted charms to keep the compartment safe. Malice looked out of the window as the train sped past foggy fields and dingy hamlets and wondered where Seth

was. Knowing Seth, he was probably driving Maniacal mad with overly enthusiastic questions. The thought of this made her smile, but only for a moment.

At last, the view became nothing but trees, so many and so dense that they cut out the light of the glow-worm sky above. The train slowed and pulled into the station at the heart of the Wild Witch Woods with a triumphant whistle. Hundreds of witches streamed out on to the platform like an army of black ants and scurried into the woods beyond. Malice, Uncle Vex and Belladonna followed the crowd. The woods were thick and dark, the tall pines reaching up so high their tops were invisible. The ground beneath their feet was bouncy with fallen pine needles and moss, but aside from the witches hurrying along the well-worn path, all seemed quiet.

"It doesn't look as though Maniacal is here," said Belladonna.

"Which is exactly what he'd like you to think," said

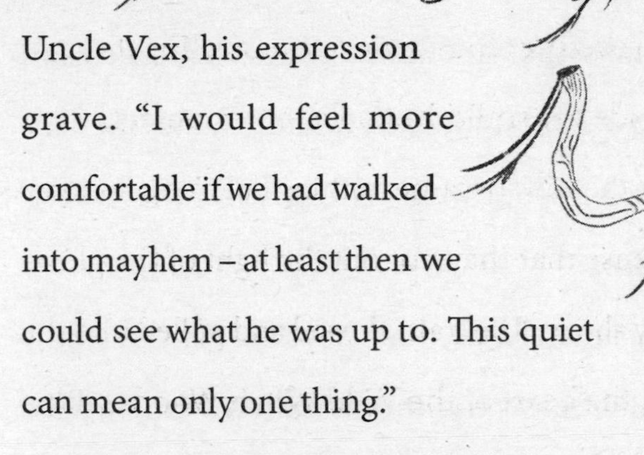

Uncle Vex, his expression grave. "I would feel more comfortable if we had walked into mayhem – at least then we could see what he was up to. This quiet can mean only one thing."

"And what is that?" asked Belladonna.

"That he is watching us and waiting, like a cat stalking its prey."

Malice scanned the trees either side of the path and shuddered at the idea of Maniacal out there somewhere, spying on them. As she continued to look, she noticed something else. There was something wrong with the trees. They looked wizened and brittle, one might even have said they looked gaunt.

Malice reached out and brushed her hand along one of the trunks; the bark flaked away at her touch and turned to dust that flittered to the ground like ash.

"There's something wrong with the trees," said Malice.

"Unfortunately, we don't have the time to worry about the trees at the moment," said Uncle Vex. "First we have to save ghost-kind from our lunatic relative."

But Malice couldn't help but worry about the trees; she could almost hear their dry dusty cries on the breeze. If Maniacal was stalking them, waiting to exact his revenge upon the witches who had trapped him two centuries before, then what better way to expose them than to destroy the very woods in which they sought sanctuary?

As they walked further into the darkness of the dense woods, Malice found herself joined by the creatures of the night. Two foxes padded

contentedly along beside her and a cloud of ghost moths clustered above her head, despite being snapped at by a grumpy tawny owl, which made itself at home on her shoulder. Three baby bats nestled in her hair, chattering excitedly about what was happening in the woods.

The Weary Necromancer hotel came into view. Its turrets loomed high above the forest floor and candles flickered warm golden light out into the gloom from a hundred windows and arrow slits. More candles lit the winding path that led to the

grand hotel entrance, and despite the stone faces of grizzly gargoyles and demented angels which seemed to rear out from every elaborately carved

cornice and gable, it was a welcoming sight.

Malice and her new friends entered the hotel. Unlike Topside, where creatures of the night are

shy of humans, in Underland no one bats an eyelid if you have bats in your hair or are flanked by foxes.

The hotel lobby, like the ghost train before it, was wall to wall with witches. The sounds of doors slamming, witches cackling and cauldrons clanking filled the air. To Malice's left, a set of double doors with a sign which read "Meditation" opened into a room packed with witches sitting cross-legged on the floor, chanting spells which made the air around them pulse. Malice felt an odd sensation – like cobwebs drifting on to her skin.

"Protection charms," said a familiar voice in her ear. "They're working to keep Maniacal's mayhem out of the hotel so that we can focus on defeating him. We lose our strength when we lose our unity."

Malice spun round to see her nana smiling at her.

"Nana!" Malice threw her arms around her, which sent the owl squawking indignantly into the air.

Nana's face had the same propensity for scowling

as Ma's, but Nana chose to smile instead.

"Now, let me look at you," said Nana.

The owl had resumed its place on Malice's shoulder and pecked at Nana's fingers as she checked behind her ears.

"Still washing behind those ears, I see," Nana said disapprovingly. "Would it hurt you to let just a couple of earwigs nest behind them? Spare a thought for the wildlife, dear."

Malice pulled a face.

"Nana, what's wrong with the trees?"

"The trees? What do you mean, my crusty pustule? We've been so busy here since Maniacal returned, I've not had a moment to step outside."

"They don't look right, or feel right," said Malice. "They seem … drained."

Nana frowned.

"We should take a look," said Nana, and they were about to head outside together, when Belladonna

stepped in front of them. Her face was alive with an excitement that Malice had never seen in the serene, unruffled tearoom owner. Uncle Vex was by her side, looking anxious.

"Who makes these?" Belladonna asked urgently, leading Nana across the lobby to a glass cabinet.

The cabinet was full of jewellery for sale: amulets of deadly nightshade flowers encased in amber, hung from silver chains, and ornate mourning brooches with the same poisonous purple flowers in their centres, lay on small black silk pillows.

"A local lady," said Nana. "She wears a mourning veil, so I have never actually seen her face, but she goes by the name of Toxicana Heartsick."

Belladonna swayed where she stood and Vex took her arm to steady her.

"Do you know where she lives?" Belladonna asked, a note of desperation in her voice.

"I think she lives near where the cave mine ghouls

have their settlement," said Nana. "That would explain her access to such lovely amber. It comes from the trees, you know."

"I have to go," said Belladonna to Malice and Uncle Vex. "I'm sorry." And she began to weave her way through the crowds of witches back towards the hotel entrance.

"Belladonna, wait!" called Malice, chasing after her. "I don't think it's safe out there, there's something wrong with the trees!"

"Please, Belladonna!' called Uncle Vex. "I really think you should stay here."

But Belladonna kept on running, past reception and out of the hotel. Malice hesitated, weighing up the odds, between who needed her more right now – the five-hundred-strong coven in the hotel, or Belladonna alone in the Wild Witch Woods. Malice chose the latter and gave chase. *Besides,* she thought to herself as she ran, *Seth isn't at the hotel, he's most*

likely being held in the woods somewhere, so I might as well be out here on the lookout.

Malice heard footsteps behind her. Her uncle was following, muttering through laboured breaths: "What's wrong with staying in the nice hotel full of witches and small triangular sandwiches?"

Malice smiled to herself as her boots crunched over dead leaves and sank into soft bracken; if her uncle would rather stay in the hotel with the witches, he must be *really* scared of the woods! Once Uncle Vex had caught up to her, they ran together, following the swish of Belladonna's ballgown through the dense bank of trees. The creatures that had befriended Malice remained by her side and above her head as she ran.

They were in the thickest part of the woods now and the quiet was conspicuous. Woods were never quiet; they were a cacophonous orchestra of animals, insects and birds, big and small, all singing

their songs as loudly as they could. But not here. The fragile trees were not the only thing worrying Malice. What could have happened to terrify the woodland creatures into silence?

They ran on, until the trees began to thin, revealing steep rocky cliffs climbing up towards the sky ahead of them. The black glisten of Belladonna's gown perpetually disappearing around trees a few steps in front of them.

"This was not part of the plan!" gasped Uncle Vex.

"We didn't have a plan," puffed Malice. "So, who knows, this might have been our plan all along."

"I seriously doubt it," said Uncle Vex, ducking under a low branch that threatened to knock his hat off. "*I* had planned to plan the plan whilst indulging in a hot-bone massage, followed by a fox-poo facial, followed by teeny tiny maggot cakes on a silver cake stand."

Belladonna stopped suddenly and Malice, with her

menagerie and Uncle Vex skidded to a halt behind her.

"You whine like a bobcat," Belladonna said to Uncle Vex, who scowled at her. "Here," Belladonna continued, pointing to the dark cave set into the rocks like a great yawning mouth. "This is where the cave mine ghouls live."

Uncle Vex leaned over her shoulder and said quietly:

"Cave mine ghouls are not famous for their hospitality and they don't take kindly to surprise visitors. There is a protocol for approaching a cave mine…"

Belladonna ignored him and strode confidently into the clearing.

A brilliant flash of light, followed by a canon-strength gust of air and smoke, knocked Belladonna clean off her hobnail boots. Malice ran to help her up and Uncle Vex followed mumbling "Nobody ever listens to the investigator! Oh, no, you just go ahead and make your own rules."

"Are you OK?" asked Malice.

Belladonna patted herself down, coughing in the thick smoke.

"Yes, thank you. I'm fine."

"Malice?" came a voice through the cloud.

"Seth?" Malice called. "Is that you?"

Malice squinted into the creamy cloud and was rewarded by seeing Seth's face squinting back at her from the entrance to the cave.

“It *is* you!” she squealed.

The two friends ran at each other and hugged tightly.

“What happened to you?” asked Malice. “I’ve been so worried!”

“Maniacal tied me to a tree while he went off to cause some mayhem. He said my ‘incessant questions’ were driving him mad. Toxicana found me and brought me back to her cave. It is so cool in there! And she’s friends with all the cave ghouls, who look pretty awful, but actually they’re really nice ghouls once you get to know them.”

“I’m so happy you’re OK!” said Malice.

“Me too, old chap,” said Uncle Vex, clapping Seth on the back. “Really wouldn’t do to have lost you on your first Underland mission.”

Malice recalled that her uncle had an unfortunate habit of losing his apprentices during investigations.

“Where is Ms Toxicana Heartsick?” Uncle Vex

continued. "I'd like to thank her myself for rescuing one of my protégés."

Malice reached into her pocket and pulled out Seth's protection lanyard. She placed it back around his neck and breathed a little easier for the first time since that morning.

Just then, she noticed a tall figure emerging through the smoke.

"Toxicana!" called Seth. "These are my friends. Malice, Vexatious and…"

"Belladonna!" said a tall, regal-looking woman, pulling back a thick mourning veil to reveal long white hair, which fell in waves down her elegant ballgown, and a face almost identical to Belladonna's.

"Strychnine," said Belladonna.

"Strychnine?" said Seth. "I thought your name was Toxicana."

"I changed my name," said Strychnine. "It was easier to begin again as someone else. My name held

too many painful memories."

"I searched for you," said Belladonna.

"I didn't want to be found," replied Strychnine.

"I wanted to tell you I was sorry. I know you didn't try to steal Gregor. As soon as I realized that Maniacal had used his pocket watch to trick us, I tried to find you to tell you I was wrong," said Belladonna. "But you'd gone."

"I thought you hated me," said Strychnine.

"Never!" said Belladonna, clutching her heart. "Do you hate *me* for doubting you?"

"Never!" said Strychnine. "But why are you here?"

"To stop Maniacal Malign," said Belladonna. "To ensure no sisters lose each other to his lies ever again."

Strychnine and Belladonna glided towards one another and threw their arms around each other, twirling and whirling in a tornado of grey and black satin. Uncle Vex blew his nose hard into his handkerchief and wiped his eyes on his sleeve.

"It's so beautiful," he sobbed. "Reunited, after two centuries."

Malice and Seth grinned at each other and at the two sisters kicking up dust and leaves as they danced together. It was a beautiful moment. Until a creaking scream split the air, followed by a splintering crash which made the ground shudder as an ancient tree fell to the ground, dead.

IT WOULD BE BRILLIANT WERE IT NOT SO HEINOUS

"I told you something was wrong with the trees!" said Malice.

They were standing around a giant pine tree lying on the ground, its brown needles still fluttering around in the air as though confused by what had just happened.

"This makes no sense," said Uncle Vex. "This tree is dry as bone. It's been completely desiccated."

Malice ran round to the root end.

"From the bottom up," she said. "These roots look as though they haven't seen rain for years."

"This is a problem that some of the cave ghouls and I have been trying to remedy," said Strychnine sadly. "Balms, potions, compresses; we've tried them all and still the trees die."

It was then that Malice noticed a pipe sticking out of the muddy tangle, cleverly designed to look like part of the root system. She brushed away the dirt and saw that the pipe led along the ground and joined another disguised pipe at the base of another tree.

"There's something weird going on here," Malice called.

She was joined by the others, along with the nosey night creatures who had taken to following her everywhere. They began to search the woodland floor, crouched over and brushing the pine needles and cones aside as they went. Once their eyes had tuned into what they were looking for, the camouflaged

pipes became easy to find. Soon they had unearthed a whole network of pipes, running right the way through the wood, connected to every single tree.

"Someone is sucking the life out of the trees," said Uncle Vex incredulously. "I've never seen such an audacious scheme!"

"But why?" asked Seth.

"And who?" asked Malice.

"Could it be the cave mine ghouls?" Uncle Vex pondered.

"No, definitely not," said Strychnine. "They love trees. They are as devastated as I am that the Wild Witch Woods are dying. The trees of today are their amber finds of the future. Amber is made from hardened tree resin; the cave ghouls rely on it for their livelihoods. And besides, the ghouls would never be so wantonly wicked."

"I think we all know who *would* do something so wicked," said Belladonna.

"Maniacal," said Malice.

The others nodded their heads gravely.

"We need to follow these pipes," said Malice.

It wasn't easy in the maze of trees and encroaching dusk to find which direction the pipes were going in; it was like trying to trace one snake in a nest of vipers. But eventually they discovered a small winding path off the main track through the woods, along which the pipes – covered over with leaves and twigs – seemed to wend. Malice realized they had been running all over them when they were chasing Belladonna, quite oblivious to what was beneath their feet.

They followed the path for some time. Each member of the team kept as quiet as possible, speaking in hushed tones if they had to speak at all. Maniacal might suddenly spring out from anywhere.

"The pipes are leading us closer to the hotel," hissed Malice.

"Yes," whispered Uncle Vex. "That's been worrying me too."

The smoke rising out from the chimneys of The Weary Necromancer was just coming into view above the tops of the trees when Malice spotted something in the canopy not far ahead. She tugged at Uncle Vex's sleeve and pointed. He squinted up into the trees and silently gestured to the others to halt.

A figure was sitting cross-legged on a large bough, high up in a towering pine tree.

"Is that Rumpelstiltskin?" Seth whispered close to Malice's ear.

Malice shook her head. Even from this distance she could make out the clumpy greasy hair and the pinched weasel face she recognized from the portrait back at Malignant House. His mouth was twisted into a sneer which made Malice's blood run cold.

"No," Malice whispered back. "That is Maniacal Malign."

They tiptoed on, the pipework beneath their feet becoming thicker and thicker, the closer they got. In the near distance was a clearing. Malice spotted it first and her gasp caused the others to follow her gaze.

The pipes ran like vines along the clearing and up into the biggest cauldron Malice had ever seen. The cauldron was the size of a cottage, and whatever the pipes were pumping into it was glooping loudly inside

the giant cast-iron cooking pot. A thick hose snaked up out of the middle and Malice followed its ascent with her eyes, up, up, up, into the pine tree, where Maniacal Malign held it with both hands, the wide nozzle of the hose trained on the roof of the hotel.

Malice crouched down and sifted amongst the woodland debris for something sharp. Her fingers touched upon a small piece of jagged rock. She picked it up and began to scratch at one of the pipes with it. The others knelt down to watch. After a minute of hard scratching, the rock tore a thin hole in the pipe. A trickle of sticky resin bubbled out of the hole and dripped on to the ground. Malice looked back over to the hose curling up out of the cauldron. A thick bulge had begun slowly rising up the pipe, like a racoon trying to fight its way out of a python's body after being swallowed.

Maniacal Malign was draining the trees in the wood of all their resin. *No wonder they look so sickly!*

Malice thought. The question was *why*.

Suddenly, like the clicking of a combination lock when the wheels inside the mechanism line up, Malice unlocked Maniacal Malign's plan for revenge.

"I know what he's doing!" hissed Malice.

"The cave ghouls helped the witches seal Maniacal's pocket watch in amber, right?"

Uncle Vex nodded.

"This is his revenge!" Malice went on. "First, he kills all the trees that the cave ghouls love so much. And then he lures the witches back to scene of the crime. Think about it. He has half the witches in Underland squeezed into The Weary Necromancer. And now he's going to cover the whole hotel in resin. He is going to seal the witches inside for ever, like they sealed up his pocket watch. One hotel-sized amber prison."

"An audacious plan!" said Belladonna. "It would be brilliant were it not so heinous."

"Yes," mused Uncle Vex. "As is so often the way with Underland criminal capers."

"He could pretty much wipe out any opposition to his time tyranny in one foul, sticky swoop," said Malice.

"Or gloop," said Seth. "Look at the size of that cauldron; imagine how many thousands of gallons of resin must be in there."

"But would it really seal them in the hotel for ever?" Uncle Vex pondered.

"I've climbed a lot of trees," said Seth. "Trust me, it's sticky stuff. Just trying to get even the tiniest bit of sap off your hands is hard enough. Imagine being rained on by the resin of a thousand trees!"

"I take your point," said Uncle Vex. He touched his hand to his quiff, as though to reassure it that he would let no resin near it.

"So, what now?" asked Strychnine. Her eyes followed the bulge of resin in its slow climb towards

the top of the hose. By now several more bulges had joined it, all oozing their way up the pipe, with still more following behind, as the resin inside the cauldron was sucked up.

"Well, we need to stop him, that's for sure," said Uncle Vex. "But he's still got that bally watch on him, and if we try anything, he can just turn it on us!"

Seth looked at the tawny owl sitting on a branch just above Malice's head.

"Do you think you could ask your owl friend to help us?" he asked.

"I should think so," said Malice. "What do you have in mind?"

"I'll climb the tree. Then, when I give the signal, you get your owl to steal the watch out of Maniacal's pocket, and while he's distracted I'll grab the hose off him and chuck it down to you guys."

"Can't let you do it, old chap," said Uncle Vex. "It's too risky."

"Do *you* want to do it?" asked Malice.

"In these trousers?" Uncle Vex looked appalled.

"I can try," said Belladonna. "It's been a while since I climbed a tree, but..."

"Look," said Seth. "I don't want to blow my own trumpet but there are two things I'm really good at. One of them is riding a bike and the other is climbing trees. My dads say I could climb a tree before I could walk."

Malice could well believe it. She was a pretty good tree climber herself, but she was an amateur compared to Seth.

Uncle Vex pulled a face like he'd just mistakenly eaten a rabbit poo instead of a raisin, but he really had no time to argue the point. Even from this distance they could all see the hose pulsating with the force of the resin pushing up towards the nozzle. Uncle Vex nodded resignedly.

Malice beckoned to the owl, who flew gracefully over and landed on her shoulder. She asked the tawny

owl very nicely – owls are sticklers for manners – if it would mind removing the pocket watch from Maniacal's pocket. The owl agreed. It trained its large round eyes on the glint of gold protruding out of Maniacal's waistcoat and waited for Seth's signal.

"All right, Seth" said Malice. "Go. We'll be waiting."

"Be careful, young Seth," said Strychnine, ruffling Seth's hair.

Seth grinned. Then he turned and ran lightly over the mossy floor, and with the speed and agility of a squirrel, he began to climb the tall pine tree in which Maniacal was balanced.

"Ahh, they grow up so fast," said Strychnine, as Belladonna linked her arm through hers.

Malice watched Seth climb the tree. Her heart was beating so loudly, she was sure that

Maniacal must hear it. It was a long way up and Malice could feel herself clenching her teeth with nerves.

Finally, he reached the topmost branches. Maniacal was sitting on the end of a thick branch that directly overlooked the hotel. Slowly, and with a ballet dancer's grace, Seth began to sidle along Maniacal's branch. The first glob had reached the end of the hose and the others had risen to join it, so that the hose bulged, stretching and creaking under the pressure of thousands of gallons of resin being forced up through the pipe. From her position below, Malice could see Maniacal's whole body shaking from the hose's violent vibrations as he worked to unlock the nozzle, ready to fire. She could only imagine Seth's view of the caramel-coloured resin swirling around inside the giant cauldron below him, and hoped with all her might that he didn't slip and fall in.

Seth looked down at Malice and gave the thumbs up. Malice gave the word to the owl and the great

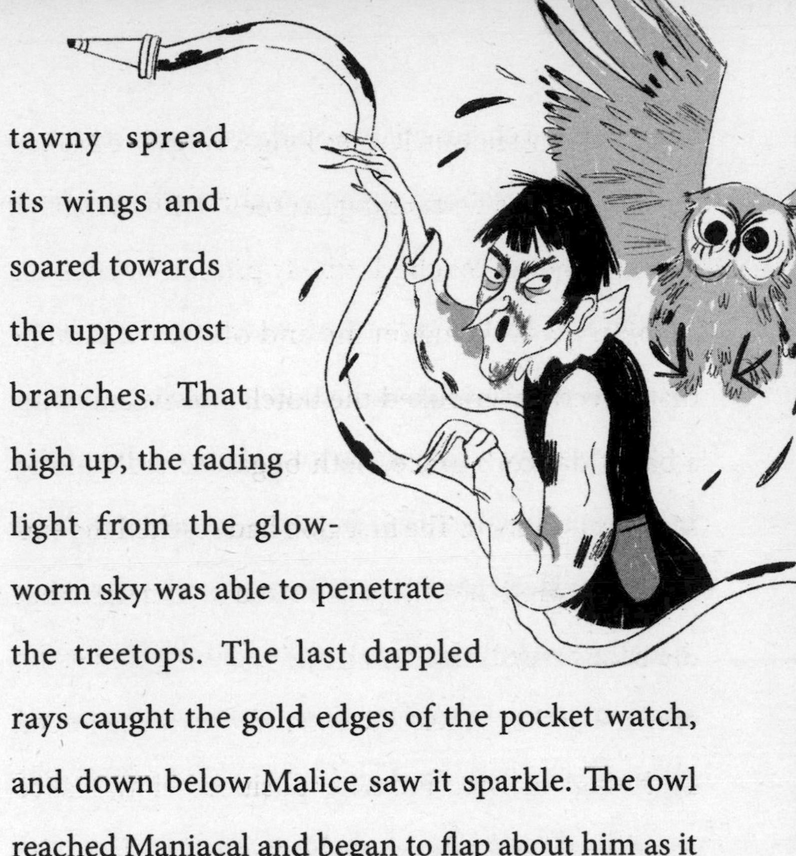

tawny spread its wings and soared towards the uppermost branches. That high up, the fading light from the glow-worm sky was able to penetrate the treetops. The last dappled rays caught the gold edges of the pocket watch, and down below Malice saw it sparkle. The owl reached Maniacal and began to flap about him as it angled its talons towards the watch in his waistcoat pocket. Maniacal began to shout and hit out at the bird, knocking at it with the end of the hose. The owl ducked his attack and plucked the watch from the pocket but seemed unable to fly away. Malice saw something glinting and realized that the watch must be attached to his waistcoat by a chain. The owl

tugged at the chain, but it wouldn't come lose.

Maniacal grabbed at the watch, the heavy hose tucked underarm.

"Oh no!" Malice exclaimed, watching as Maniacal fumbled with the watch. "He's going to stop time."

Seth, seeing what was about to happen, launched himself at the ghost and began to wrestle the hose from Maniacal. Maniacal screamed with rage, as he was attacked by both the owl trying to steal his watch and Seth trying to steal his hose. The time-tampering ghost shoved Seth hard.

"Whoa!" cried Seth, as he landed hard on his back across the branch. But Maniacal wasn't finished with him yet. Still lugging the heavy hose under one arm and punching at the owl with the other, Maniacal aimed a kick at Seth. Quick as a flash, Seth rolled off the branch, grabbing the hose as he did so, and dived into the air.

He fell for a few heart-stopping seconds before the

hose caught over a branch, and Seth was left swinging in the trees like Tarzan – if Tarzan had been wearing a doublet and hose. Maniacal lunged for the hose, but he missed his footing. He stumbled backwards,

his legs kicking out wildly like a man balancing on a barrel. The owl gave one last almighty tug and the chain broke free, just as Maniacal lost his balance.

With arms flailing and curses flying out of his mouth, Maniacal Malign tumbled down through the tree, hitting every branch on the way down, and landed headfirst with a thick *splosh* in the giant cauldron of resin.

"Seth!" Malice cried. "Hold on!"

"You got it!" called Seth, who was swinging back and forth among the trees as he held tightly on to the hose.

The vat of resin made plopping-fart sounds as Maniacal sank further and further towards the bottom of the cauldron.

The owl returned and dropped the watch into Malice's outstretched hand.

Malice thanked the owl and pocketed the watch. She had bigger things to worry about right then than a time-stopping pocket watch; she needed to get Seth back down on to terra firma.

"Wait there, Seth!" called Strychnine.

"I am!" shouted Seth. "I'm not sure what makes you all think I'm planning to let go."

Strychnine pulled a small funnel-shaped horn from her pocket and blew into it. The noise was low and eerie and seemed to echo around the woods. Presently there came the rustling sound of many heavy feet on the woodland floor, and short muscular ghouls began to appear between the trees and march into the clearing.

They were a stern-faced bunch, with hooked noses and chins which bent upwards almost to meet them, and long, thick hair pulled back into ponytails. Their hands and boiler suits were black with dirt and their heavy boots looked like they'd seen some mileage.

"These are the cave mine ghouls," said Strychnine. "My faithful friends these many years."

The ghouls' expressions softened at Strychnine's words.

"You blew the danger horn," said a gruff ghoul, with an axe over his shoulder. "It had better be serious."

"It is serious," said Strychnine. "Seth is stuck, he needs your help to get safely down."

The cave ghoul grunted.

"Why is this boy's fate our concern?" he asked.

Strychnine pointed to the pipes leading up into the cauldron.

"Because he and his friends discovered who has been killing the trees," she said. "And they have stopped him."

The cave mine ghouls followed the trail of the pipes. Malice watched as they took in the scene before them, their faces a picture of sadness at the heinous misuse of their beloved trees and relief that finally

there was an answer to why the trees were dying. The ghouls crushed their faces against the dry dusty bark and wrapped their arms around the trunks, whispering soothing words.

"Ahem!" coughed Seth. "I don't mean to be a bother, but I'd really like to get down from here!"

The ghouls sprang into action. A particularly stout ghoul rooted himself to a spot beneath Seth, and then one by one the ghouls stood on each other's shoulders, until they were a tall, swaying tower balanced twenty ghouls high. The ghoul at the top of the pile held tight to Seth's waist, while he let go of the hose. Slowly and awkwardly, Seth climbed down the ghoul ladder until, at last, his feet were back on the ground.

Malice, Uncle Vex, Belladonna and Strychnine rushed to Seth and patted and hugged him and checked for injury. When they were satisfied that their friend was unharmed after his ordeal, bar a small tear in his doublet, they thanked the cave ghouls.

“Can you save the trees?” Malice asked. “Is there a way you can reverse the process and put the resin back into them?”

The ghouls were already inspecting the labyrinth of pipework leading through the woods and into the cauldron.

“It’s doable,” said one of the ghouls, rubbing his bristly face. “But it’s going to take the trees a while to recover.”

“I’ll make healing balms and root food to replenish them,” said Strychnine. “I have everything I need in my cave.”

“I’ll help you,” said Belladonna.

The sisters looked at each other, smiling, and Malice knew their years of loneliness were at an end.

“And what do we do about Maniacal?” asked Uncle Vex.

Belladonna, with the ease of an ariel acrobat, scaled one of the long pipes hanging over the side

of the giant cauldron and looked inside. Then she shimmied back down and dusted off her hands.

"I don't think we need to worry about Maniacal Malign anytime soon," she said dryly as she checked over her long fingernails to make sure none had been snagged in the climb. "He has found himself on, how would Vexatious put it? Something of a sticky wicket."

Uncle Vex nodded appreciatively and said: "Bravo!"

"I have an idea," said Malice, "of how to put an end to the bad behaviour of Maniacal and his pocket watch."

Malice ran over to a group of cave ghouls and they huddled around her for several minutes as she spoke animatedly with them, her arms waving and making shapes in the air, while the cave ghouls nodded and murmured in gruff agreement. Seth and Uncle Vex looked on in quiet interest.

"Do you know what she's up to, old chap?" asked Uncle Vex.

"Beats me," said Seth. "But if I know Malice, it'll be worth the wait."

Malice came bounding back over.

"Right," she said. "Let's get back to the hotel."

IT'S OUR MISCHIEF OR NO MISCHIEF

Back at the hotel, Nana had spread the word about what had happened and gathered all the witches out on to the front lawn in the late worm-light. They were a noisy, cackly sort of gathering and Uncle Vex looked a little green about the gills, but Malice was used to witches, and Seth was delighted.

The three investigators sat around a wooden picnic bench and the crones crowded around them like a wall of witches. The time-tampering pocket watch was laid in the middle of the table. The witches eyed it, some with contempt and some with secret longing, which only strengthened Malice's resolve to dispose of the dastardly thing.

Nana shushed the witches, and everybody leaned in closer to listen.

"Malice has something to say," Nana said, and nodded to Malice.

"The way I see it," Malice began. "The only way to dispose of this watch is to dismantle it and hide it in as many different locations as possible."

There was a flurry of positive murmurs from the crowd.

"Unfortunately, this isn't fool-proof. Even if a hundred of us took a piece each and hid it, there will always be some treasure hunter..."

"Probably from your family!" shouted one witch and snorts of laughter rippled through the crowd.

"Well, yes," said Malice, putting her hands up in surrender. "I wouldn't put it past them. But there will always be some treasure hunter or power-hungry ghost who will stop at nothing to find all the scattered watch pieces and put it back together again. And that would put everyone who had hid a part of the mechanism at risk."

This time the combined shiver of half a thousand witches washed through the crowd like a cold breeze.

"Tempestuous and Turbulence have spent the last two centuries in exile for fear of that very occurrence," piped up Nana, and everyone nodded.

Malice was grateful for Nana's command of the crowd.

"So, what's your plan?" asked a witch with a silver chain that went from her nose to her ear.

"I suggest that we dismantle the watch, turn our

backs and ask the night creatures to each take a piece away with them and hide it somewhere they know no one will ever look."

"Why are we turning our backs?" asked a witch with dreadlocks.

"So that we don't know which night creature has taken which piece," said Uncle Vex. "None of us will ever know who took what where. If there are no witnesses, we are all safe, and the watch remains lost for ever." Uncle Vex finished with a flourish and found himself the recipient of more than a few admiring glances and batted eyelids from the witches surrounding them.

"How are we going to dismantle it without damaging the magic?" asked a witch in a floral hijab.

"I will do it," said Strychnine, who had just arrived. She glided into the centre of the conference and laid her jewellery-making wallet out across the table. "My hand is steady, and I am skilled at dealing with

delicate jewellery items."

Strychnine sat down at the bench and pulled the watch towards her. She opened it gently – to a sharp intake of breath amongst everyone present – and began.

They watched her, fascinated, as she proceeded to dismantle the delicate innards and workings of the pocket watch. It was a slow and careful business. Belladonna stood by her side and acted as her assistant, passing her sister the fine screwdrivers and tiny tweezers as she asked for them. The last of the light was swallowed by the night and still they worked. Nana used the end of her wand to light the intricate mechanisms beneath Strychnine's careful fingers.

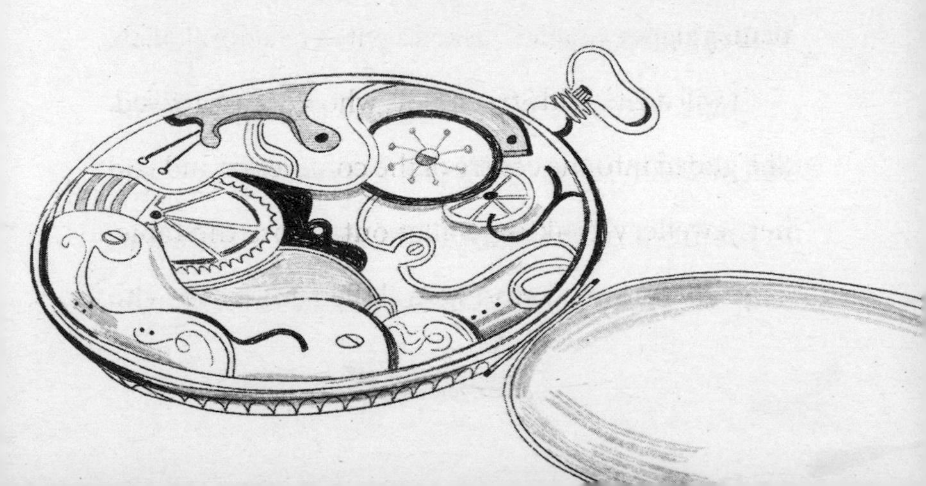

By the time she had finished it was fully dark, and the witches at the front of the group held candles to light the table. Spread out across the wooden bench was a mass of miniscule cogs and screws. Somewhere in amongst all those singular items was the time bending magic that Maniacal had created, though it was impossible to tell in which piece or pieces the magic was embedded.

Strychnine stood carefully and stretched her back. "Your turn," she said to Malice, smiling.

Malice walked to the edge of the bench and met the eyes of many hundreds of expectant witches.

"Would everyone who can moth whisper or commune with night creatures please step forward," Malice called.

There was much shuffling and elbowing as the witches with these particular gifts made their way to the front of the crowd and joined Malice and Seth around the table. A hush ran through the

gathering as, using their unique chants, the creature charmers invited their friends to join them. For a few moments nothing stirred. And then the air was filled with a susurration like crisp leaves gusting on an autumn day, and the grass rustled with a sound like October drizzle.

A shimmering nebulous mass of moths, bats and owls hovered above the crowd, while, below, a legion of tiny beasts scurried over hobnailed boots and around broomsticks before scaling the legs of the picnic table. When all the creatures had gathered, Nana raised her arms and addressed the crowd of witches.

"Let us turn away now and allow our friends to remove Maniacal Malign's monstrous mechanics from our midst once and for ever!"

As one, the whole congregation turned their backs to the table; many closed their eyes too, to be sure they had no idea where the pieces might go.

There came a fluttering of wings, the pitter-patter of tiny feet and the delicate tinkle of golden watch pieces being taken up by spindly legs and mandibles. Then, with a beating of multiple wings – which sounded like the wind whipping at the sails of a ghost ship – the creatures of the air rose into the night, a cloud of silver and black against the dark sky. And the fauna – the creatures of the earth – vanished in a scuttling rustle into the long grass, the clickety-clack of a million teeny legs fading into the distance as they scattered themselves and the watch pieces in a hundred different directions.

When the air and earth was quiet once more, everybody turned back to the table to find it empty; not a single cog remained. Maniacal Malign's watch was gone.

A cheer went up and instantly firework messages were sent out across the skies of Underland to let the inhabitants know that Maniacal's reign of time terror

was over. Nana declared that a party was just the thing to celebrate, and the witches wasted no time setting their cauldrons to bubble with pumpkin punch and butternut squash chilli con carne; mouldy of course. Malice spotted the shop-witches from the Be-Careful-What-You-Wish-For Emporium, Blight, Miasma and Pestilence, setting up a skiffle band under the pergola in front of the hotel.

"Malice Morbid Malign," said Blight.

"The girl who rescued time," said Miasma.

"A vanquisher of crime," added Pestilence.

"Hello," said Malice. "I got your note."

"You were meant to," said Miasma.

"You know, you could have just told me you'd come here. You didn't need to make it so cryptic."

The shop witches looked at Malice as though she'd just cleaned their cauldrons.

"And where's the fun in that, I'd like to know?" asked Blight.

"Topunders! They're all the same," Pestilence tutted. "Always looking for the easiest route."

"Aren't you going to introduce us to your friend?" asked Miasma, looking over at Seth. There was a twinkle in her eye that Malice didn't much like the look of. Nor did she like the way Blight was twirling her wand and licking her lips.

"I don't think so," said Malice. "Not today." And she hurried back over to where Nana was chatting to Uncle Vex and checking behind Seth's ears.

"Will you stay for the party, Malice, my little dung beetle?" asked Nana.

"I'd like to," said Malice. "But we really ought to get back. Seth and I have got school tomorrow."

"Tsk!" Nana exclaimed. "School indeed. You're just like your grandad."

Malice grinned; that was one of the nicest things anyone had ever said to her.

"By the way," said Uncle Vex. "What were you talking to the cave ghouls about in the woods?"

"Oh yes!" said Malice. "I almost forgot."

Malice put two fingers in her mouth and gave a whistle. The trees began to rustle and there was the sound of wooden wheels being pushed along the ground. Presently a cart came into view, pushed by several cave ghouls. Standing on top of the cart, looking apoplectic with rage, was Maniacal Malign, completely sealed inside a solid block of amber, which had been very nicely smoothed to a shine and sealed in a glass case.

The cave ghouls wheeled the Amber block over to where Malice, Seth, Uncle Vex and Nana stood.

"Thanks, guys," said Malice. "This looks even

better than I imagined!"

The cave ghouls grunted in an appreciative sort of way. Cave ghouls were not ones for great shows of emotion.

"It wasn't that hard," grumbled a ghoul with a set of welding goggles on his head. "The tree resin did most of the work for us. He won't be causing anyone any more trouble."

"Let's hope not," said Malice. She turned to Nana. "I thought this time, rather than banish Maniacal, it might be better to keep an eye on him."

"It's a marvellous idea, Malice," said Nana. "I know just where to keep him!"

Nana escorted the cave ghouls into the hotel. The amber block, with Maniacal gurning with anger inside it, was heaved up on to a plinth in the lobby, next to Strychnine's jewellery display cabinet.

"Now everyone can keep an eye on him," said Nana.

"Awesome!" said Seth.

Malice said goodbye to Nana and Seth promised to show her his comic collection when Nana next came to Malignant House for Halloween. Belladonna decided to stay in the Wild Witch Woods with Strychnine in her cave for a while because they had two hundred years to catch up on.

They left the witches' party at the hotel in full swing. There was raucous singing and dancing by the glow of the little fires that kept the cauldrons happily bubbling and the smell of singed popcorn

and roasted pumpkin in the air. Malice was sad to miss the festivities, but she and Seth really did need to get back up to Topside.

Nana let them use her express lift to the Malignant House mausoleum. One after the other they climbed inside an old grandfather clock standing in the bog-mud bath treatment room and pulled the glass case closed behind them. Uncle Vex swung the pendulum and they were catapulted upwards towards Topside at such a speed that their cheeks pulled down like bulldog jowls, and it felt as though their chins were touching their shoes.

They stepped out into the mausoleum and wearily climbed the steps from the catacombs and walked through the crypt, until at last they reached the entrance that led out into the dark gardens of Malignant House.

Malice braced herself for mayhem to still be ringing and raging through Felicity Square, but, to

her surprise, everything was quiet.

"I'm going to walk Seth back to his house," said Uncle Vex, when they reached the rusty iron gates which led out onto the street.

"I'll see you tomorrow at school," Seth yawned. "If only the other kids knew what a weekend we've had."

Malice laughed.

"They'd never believe us," she said. Malice was used to living a double life. It was nice to have Seth to share it with. "Won't your dads think it's odd that you're dressed like a Tudor?"

Seth looked down at his knitted hose and voluminous shorts.

"Nah," he said. "They'll just know I'm living my best life."

Malice watched as Uncle Vex and Seth rounded the corner, and then she took a look around Felicity Square. The cars were back on their wheels instead of their roofs and their paintwork was gleaming.

Malice frowned and walked down the alleyway to the gardens behind the houses, where so much pandemonium had been raging the morning before.

What Malice found was quite the opposite to pandemonium. Here in the back gardens, peace and tranquillity reigned once more. The crater left after Mr Snoot's garden was demolished by TNT had been filled in, and new shrubs and trees had been planted.

The plants that had been uprooted and piled on the roof had been restored to their rightful positions and, most astonishing of all, Ms Egotist's steamrollered garden had been un-rollered; the plants that had been pancake flat were now wafting gracefully in the cool night air.

"It was your parents!" came a voice.

Malice looked up to see Mr Parvenu leaning out of his bedroom window, his nightcap flapping in the breeze.

"What do you mean?" asked Malice.

"Your parents. They fixed everything. I wouldn't have believed it if I hadn't seen it with my own eyes," said Mr Parvenu. "They were out all last night, putting everything right. Nobody else saw them. But I did."

Malice stared. Could it be that her parents had taken it upon themselves to fix Maniacal's malevolent mischief?

Malice hurried back to Malignant House, where the whole family were sitting in the kitchen. Several vials of putrid bubbling liquid sat in the middle of the table.

"Ahh, Malice," said Ma. "You're back. Come over 'ere and sniff my stink bombs."

Malice sat down at the table and Ma pulled the stopper off the first vial. A thin stream of green vapour spiralled out of the top and made a brown scorch mark on the ceiling.

"Your nana sent me a ghoulagram to tell me what you'd done," said Grandad. "That's my girl. I knew

you'd put a stop to that troublesome time trickster."

"Well, I had a lot of help along the way," said Malice.

Pa covered Antipathy-Rose's ears.

"We do not use the 'H' word around the baby!" he snapped. "You keep your potty mouth in check, young lady."

Malice smiled mischievously.

"I hear you've been doing a bit of the 'H' word yourself!" she said, taking a sniff of Ma's proffered stink bomb and recoiling as her nostrils closed in protest. "Phew, that's a good one Ma," she said, her eyes watering.

Ma grinned and passed over another vial.

"We were not h-h-h..." Pa choked, he couldn't bring himself to say the word. "We were not restoring order to be on better terms with the neighbours. Felicity Square is our turf. We do the mischief around these parts. And we'll not be upstaged by some watch-wielding weasel."

"It's our mischief or no mischief," added Ma, giving Malice a wink as she turned as green as the stink-bomb she'd just smelled. "Maniacal had no right, coming round here causing trouble; that's our job!"

"Well, he won't be causing any *more* trouble," said Grandad. "Not now the Private Underland Investigators have saved the night! I'm proud of you, duck."

"Grandad," said Pa. "I do wish you'd stop encouraging Malice's do-gooding. It's embarrassing. But in this instance," he went on. "I will allow that you did g-g-g-g..."

"Don't say it, Pa," pleaded Ma. "Not in front of the baby."

"You didn't do half bad," said Pa gruffly and planted a greasy kiss on Malice's head.

Antipathy-Rose clapped her hands and went back to

gnawing on a padlock.

After smelling the rest of Ma's stink-bombs and agreeing with her that vial number four had just the right amount of fart stench and cabbage odour for the *Mischief Monthly* recipe section, Malice headed up to bed.

In the days that followed, she and Seth received regular correspondence from Uncle Vex with regard to the clean-up operation in Underland, in the aftermath of Maniacal's time torment.

Mrs Todd had managed to repair her reputation by introducing a pie which boasted twice the amount of rotten entrails as her previous offerings. Lilith and Vlad had their teeth restored to them after a farmer wrestled them out of two pumpkins which had been causing havoc in his pumpkin patch. Belladonna and Strychnine have been making up for lost time, by developing a scintillating new range of poisonous tea blends, and, much to Uncle Vex's chagrin, Belladonna

has been dating a cave ghoul named Hex. The cave ghouls managed to reverse the damage to the trees in the Wild Witch Woods, which hopefully meant the woods would be a terrifying place of shadows and witchcraft for centuries to come.

And Maniacal Malign remained, encased in amber for all to see – a stark reminder that you never mess with another mischief maker's mischief!

Malice and her ghastly family, would ~~NOT~~ like to thank:

Jenni *'mischief-maker'* Jennings, Malice's Creator

Hannah *'pesky-pest'* Peck, Malice's Illustrator

Chloe *'scallywag'* Seager, Jenni's Agent

Scholastic *(the ringleaders)*, Jenni's Publisher

Yasmin *'misbehaver'* Morrissey, Jenni's Editor

Ruth *'malcontent'* Bennett, Jenni's Supporting Editor

Andrew *'rabble-rouser'* Biscomb, Jenni's Art Director

Rachel *'rascal'* Lawston, Jenni's Designer

Lauren *'tomfoolery'* Fortune, Jenni's Fiction Publisher

Genevieve *'disobedience-diva'* Herr, Jenni's Copyeditor

Peter *'silly-scamp'* Matthews, Jenni's Editorial Manager

Harriet *'troublemaker'* Dunlea, Jenni's Publicist

Rebecca *'naughty-nuisance'* Gillies, Jenni's Marketer

Clare *'chaos-causer'* Hennessy, Jenni's Production Manager

NAME: Malice Morbid Malign

AGE: 11 3/4

PROFESSION: Mischief-Maker
& Amateur Detective.

LIKES: Reading, Bathing, Puzzles.

DISLIKES: Malevolent Mischief, Messy Bedrooms, Not Helping.

INTERESTING FACT: Malice discovered she could talk to night creatures when she fell into one of the sinking-bogs in the Malignant House grounds, aged 4, and was rescued by two barn owls and a fox named Darwin, who answered her cries for help. Once a month she hosts a moonlit supper-club for the night animals in the old icehouse near the mausoleum.

NAME: Seth Indiana Pinkerton

AGE: 11 1/4

PROFESSION: Paperboy & Amateur Detective.

LIKES: Skeletons, Cycling, Weirdness.

DISLIKES: Meanness, Ordinary, Bedtime.

INTERESTING FACT: Seth shares the same surname as Allan Pinkerton, the founder of Pinkerton's National Detective Agency in America in 1850 who hired the first ever female detective ; Kate Warne.

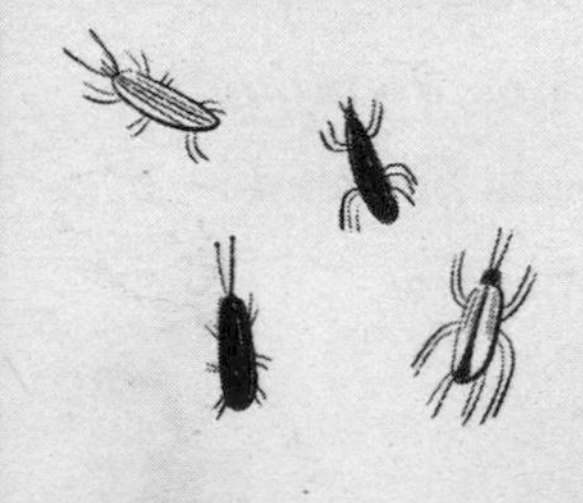

NAME: Uncle Vex (Vexatious) Malign

AGE: 58

PROFESSION: Private Underland Investigator.

LIKES: Hair gel, Sharp-suits, Righting wrongs.

DISLIKES: Injustice, Dirty fingernails, Jack-in-the-boxes.

INTERESTING FACT: Uncle Vex was once approached by MI5 to join the British intelligence team. He claims to have turned them down but Malice has her suspicions that he may occasionally help them out of a tight spot.

NAME: Ma (Tetchy-Sue) Malign

AGE: 32

(actually she is 59, but she's very sensitive about her age. Topunders have a longer life-span than Topsiders because of their magical blood.)

PROFESSION: Mischief-Maker, CEO of the Malign Haunting Agency.

LIKES: Stink bombs, Earwigs, Swag.

DISLIKES: Cleanliness, Community spirit, Recycling.

INTERESTING FACT: Ma was taught the delicate art of thievery by the ghost of Diamond Annie, a member of the infamous London all-girl gang called the Forty Elephants, who used to steal jewels and all manner of swag by stuffing it down their big bloomers and underneath their puffy crinoline dresses.

NAME: Pa (Pugnacious) Malign

AGE: 66

PROFESSION: Mischief-Maker, Director of the Malign Haunting Agency.

LIKES: Stealing, Treasure maps, Keeping eels in the bath.

DISLIKES: Books, Helping, Do-gooders.

INTERESTING FACT: In 1987 Pa broke the world record for the most flies hovering above a human head. His record was broken in 1992 by Arthropod Maggot, a Topunder from the Welsh Borders.

NAME: Grandad (Scamp) Rascally

AGE: 127

PROFESSION: Ghost, Merry Mischief-Maker.

LIKES: Poker, Stinging nettle tea, Reading.

DISLIKES: Malicious mischief,
Fuss, Thunderstorms.

INTERESTING FACT: In 1908 Grandad worked at the Grand Central Hotel in London and found himself serving breakfast one morning to Emmeline Pankhurst and her fellow suffragettes. He pretended to be polishing teapots so that he could listen to their speeches and has been a feminist ever since.

NAME: Antipathy-Rose Malign

AGE: 2

PROFESSION: Mischief-Maker & Biter.

LIKES: Biting, Deep fried pigs' ears, Escaping.

DISLIKES: Dolls with heads, Soft foods, Grown-ups who talk to her like she's a baby – even though she is a baby.

INTERESTING FACT: Antipathy-Rose ate her way through three wicker Moses baskets, four wooden cribs and a coffin, before Ma finally got her late lamented pet vultures bird cage down from the attic for her to sleep in.

NAME: Maniacal Menace Malign

AGE: 402

PROFESSION: Inventor and Mischief-Maker

LIKES: Trouble (both causing and getting into). Meanness. Poetry — surprising but true.

DISLIKES: Everyone. Friendships. Fondant Fancies.

INTERESTING FACT: Maniacal studied Errant-Engineering at the University of Underland. While there he met Daedalus — famous in Greek mythology for designing the Minotaur's labyrinth. But Maniacal's inventions were too heinous for Daedalus to stomach and they parted ways, with Daedalus threatening to build a labyrinth in which to trap Maniacal if he ever crossed his path again.

Name: Belladonna Toxiferous Nightshade

Age: 525

Profession: Owner of The Vengeful Brew on Hysteria Lane.

Likes: Growing poisonous plants. Concocting poisonous teas from poisonous plants.

Dislikes: Liars. Ballgowns without pockets. Dusting.

Interesting Fact: Since this book was written, Belladonna and Strychnine have branched out into chocolate making. They are hoping to tempt their Underland customers with their new range of Cursed-Confectionary. The truffles are created from the finest poisonous flower extracts and the most-contaminated cocoa beans money can buy. The sisters have already been featured in The Good Poisoners Guide.

NAME: Nana (Mesmerist) Rascally

AGE: 142

PROFESSION: Witch and owner of The Weary Necromancer Hotel in the Wild Witch Woods.

LIKES: Puzzle solving. Yoga. Dancing around her cauldron beneath the glow-worm sky, chanting ghost-folk songs.

DISLIKES: Disharmony. Uncharitable ghosts. Inequality.

INTERESTING FACT: Nana is the author of several successful cookbooks, including *One-Cauldron Meals for the Working Witch*, *How to Be a Culinary Crone*, and *Bake Your Way to Bedlam*. Despite being divorced, she counts Grandad Rascally as one of her best friends and he tests all her recipes before they go into her books.

Name: Lilith Phantasma Sharptooth

Age: 324

Profession: Co-owner of Lethal Legumes on Damnation Lane, with her husband Vlad.

Likes: Tofu. Knitting. Bugs — Lilith tries to encourage as many crawlies as possible into her café.

Dislikes: Scary Movies. Unkind Practical Jokes. Sunshine.

Interesting Fact: Lilith is the founder of Ghostenbury — Underland's biggest music festival. Being a well-respected musician herself (Lilith plays the double bass and drums) she has been able secure some of the biggest names in the business. Last year she booked the famous Medieval band, *Buckets of Poop* and this year she has promised ticket holders a chance to see Guy Fawkes's band, *Gunpowder Plotters*.

HAVE YOU READ?